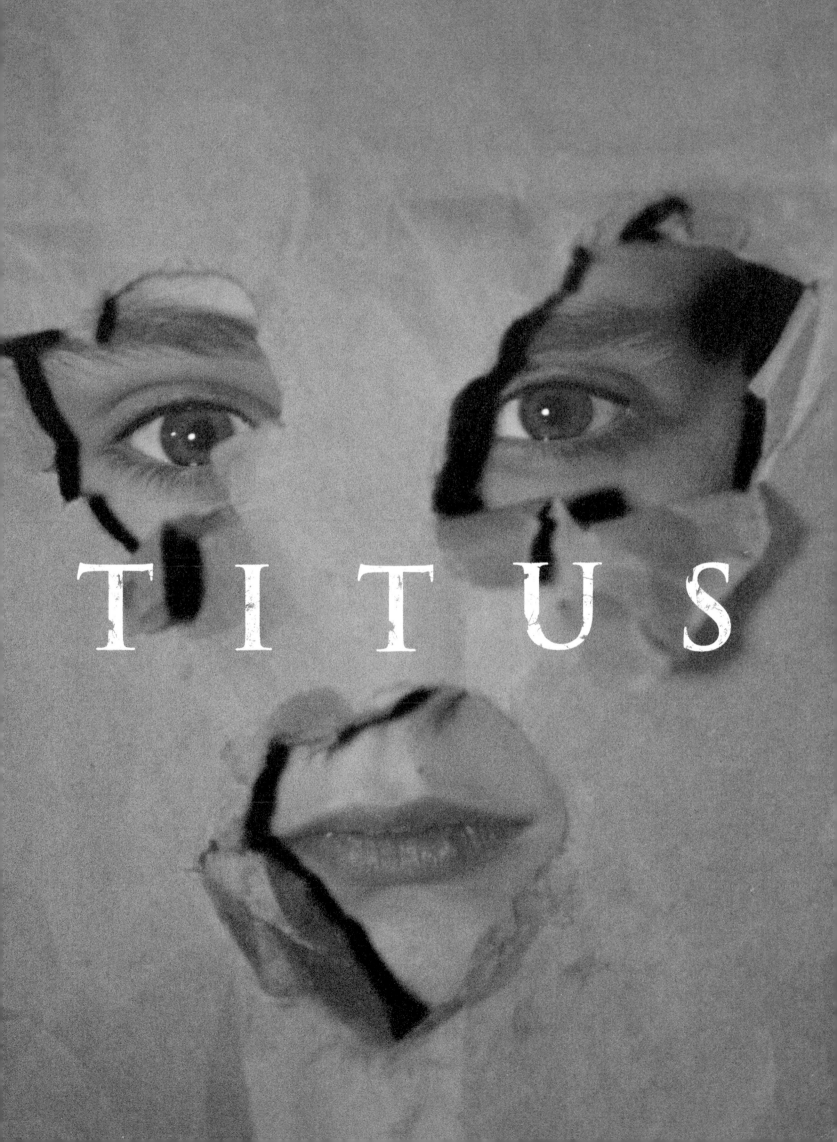

TITUS

TITUS

THE ILLUSTRATED SCREENPLAY, ADAPTED FROM
THE PLAY BY WILLIAM SHAKESPEARE

JULIE TAYMOR

A NEWMARKET PICTORIAL MOVIEBOOK

NEWMARKET PRESS
NEW YORK

For my exquisite parents, Mel and Betty,
who encouraged me to play, play, play.

Design and compilation copyright © 2000 by Newmarket Press.
Screenplay and illustrations, except where noted, copyright © 2000 by Clear Blue Sky
Productions. Movie poster on page 11, designed by Indika Entertainment
Advertising, copyright © 2000 by Overseas Filmgroup. All other photographs
copyrighted by the photographer credited.
An extension of this copyright appears on page 186.
Director's Notes copyright © 2000 by Julie Taymor.
Introduction copyright © 2000 by Jonathan Bate. Portions of
this essay originally appeared in the *New York Times.*

This book is published simultaneously in the United States of America and in Canada.

First Edition

1 3 5 7 9 10 8 6 4 2

Library of Congress Cataloging-in-Publication Data is available upon request.

ISBN 1-55704-436-8

QUANTITY PURCHASES
Companies, professional groups, clubs, and other organizations may qualify
for special terms when ordering quantities of this title. For information, write
Special Sales, Newmarket Press, 18 East 48th Street, New York, New York 10017;
call (212) 832-3575; fax (212) 832-3629; or email: sales@newmarketpress.com.
www.newmarketpress.com

Edited by Linda Sunshine   Designed by Timothy Shaner

Manufactured in the United States of America

Other Newmarket Pictorial Moviebooks Include:
The Age of Innocence: A Portrait of the Film Based on the Novel by Edith Wharton
Cradle Will Rock: The Movie and The Moment
Magnolia: The Shooting Script
The Sense and Sensibility Screenplay and Diaries
Saving Private Ryan: The Men, The Mission, The Movie
Bram Stoker's Dracula: The Film and the Legend

CONTENTS

INTRODUCTION

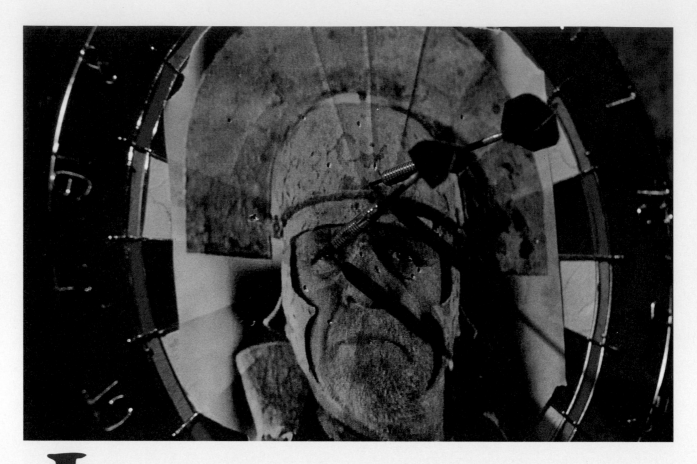

If William Shakespeare were alive today, he would be writing and directing movies. Julie Taymor's *Titus* offers a glimpse of what they might be like: challenging but accessible, tragic and comic, deeply responsive to the past yet highly relevant to the present.

Titus Andronicus was young Shakespeare's first box office smash, the work that made his name, the first of his plays to appear in print (originally published in 1594). Together with *The Spanish Tragedy* by Thomas Kyd, it established the vogue for revenge drama that lasted through *Hamlet* to the dark plays of John Webster and beyond. It has become generally known as Shakespeare's bloodiest play. But more important—and unexpectedly—it is his wittiest tragedy.

The playgoers of Elizabethan England, where the bear-baiting pit stood next to the theatre and the scaffold was a place of public entertainment, had strong stomachs for the representation of bloody revenge, dismemberment, rape and cannibalism. In our time, the rape of Lavinia and Titus' bloody banquet may seem like the sort of thing that gives Hollywood a bad name. But the violence in *Titus* is always artistically purposeful, never

showily gratuitous. There is a harsh but elegant symmetry to the action. Alarbus' limbs are lopped, and so then are Lavinia's: since Tamora Queen of the Goths loses her son, Titus General of the Romans must lose his daughter. For Julie Taymor, *Titus* belongs in more enduring company than those slick Hollywood movies in which violence is casual and unattended by feeling or afterthought.

The iconography of the movie conjures up Renaissance paintings of the martyred and the damned. This painterly quality points to two things: the visual inventiveness of Taymor's imagination, which is everywhere apparent in the film, and her belief that *Titus* is no Shakespearean potboiler, but a profound exploration of the darker recesses of humanity, a tour de force that can hold its own with the greatest and most troubling creative works of Western culture.

Ever since the time of ancient Greek tragedy, Western culture has been haunted by the figure of the revenger. He or she stands on a whole series of borderlines: between civilization and barbarity, between an individual's accountability to their own conscience and the community's need for the rule of law, between the conflicting demands of justice and mercy.

Do we have a right—a duty even—to exact revenge against those who have destroyed our loved ones? Or should we leave vengeance to the law or to the gods? And if we do take action into our own hands, are we not reducing ourselves to the same moral level as the original perpetrator of murderous deeds? Kyd began to explore these questions in *The Spanish Tragedy*; Shakespeare developed them further in *Titus Andronicus* and then raised them to their highest level in *Hamlet*.

Hieronimo in *The Spanish Tragedy* is driven mad by the death of his son. In the end his grief becomes so intense that it is literally inexpressible, causing him to bite out his own tongue. Shakespeare nods towards Hieronimo when Titus says, "Or shall we bite our tongues, and in dumb-shows / Pass the remainder of our hateful days?" The actor on the Elizabethan stage communicated with his audience in two ways: through words and gestures. When Hieronimo bites out his tongue, Kyd implies that actions speak louder than words. In *Titus*, Shakespeare picked up on this hint and pressed at the sufficiency of both language and gesture.

Shakespeare began his career as an actor, learning the elaborate rhetorical speeches and highly formalized physical gestures that characterized the relatively crude dramatic repertory of the time. The top box office star of this period, the early 1590s, was Edward Alleyn. The first Hieronimo, Alleyn was renowned for his grand style. Shakespeare, though, quickly saw the dangers of going "over the top" on stage. Working closely with his leading actor, Richard Burbage, he sought to develop a much subtler style, in which poetic language became a medium less for showy display and more for a flexible, inquiring exploration of the inner life.

Titus has its share of windy rhetorical grandiloquence—that was necessary in order to bring in the crowds. But its unique brilliance occurs in those passages where Shakespeare deliberately deprives himself of the dramatist's usual resources of word and gesture. Kyd's Hieronimo only bites himself into silence in the final scene before his death, whereas Shakespeare's Lavinia has her tongue cut out before the halfway mark in the action. For the remainder of the time, she can speak only in dumb-show. Nor can she express herself with gestures, for her hands have been cut off. She has become a visual icon of man's inhumanity to woman. So it is that her father, Titus, has to "wrest an alphabet" from the "martyr'd signs" of her mutilated body.

The revenger is driven to excess by the wrongs that he has suffered. His reaction is calculated to go beyond the original action. Titus is sent the severed heads of his sons. In response, he does not merely slit the throats of his enemy's sons—he takes their heads, grinds down the bones, bakes them in a pie and serves them to their mother for dinner. "Eat this and beat that," he might be saying.

Shakespeare's innovative discovery in *Titus Andronicus* is that extreme trauma reveals the strange proximity of horror to comedy. Titus himself gives the impression of going mad as he plans his revenge, but then he tips the audience the wink—he's only pretending to be mad; he's actually having a bit of a laugh.

Is it possible to relieve emotional anguish through language? The attempt to do so is the traditional cathartic function of poetic tragedy. In *Titus*, Marcus—the play's chief "spectator" figure—faces the appalling mutilation of his niece, Lavinia, and finds himself searching for a language of mourning that will "ease [her] misery." Her father, Titus, later tries to share her pain by holding her closely to him and comparing her to the weeping wind, himself to first the sea and then the earth. But even this elemental language is insufficient. Lavinia's woes are literally *unspeakable*. Throughout *Titus*, Shakespeare pushes at the boundaries between true expression and false, sanity and madness, speech and silence. He is intrigued by tears on the one hand and laughter on the other, because they are intensely physiological expressions of inner states.

When Titus confronts the horrific fate of his children, his brother Marcus expects him to rant in the style of Edward Alleyn. But he does not cry or curse. He laughs. Critics in the eighteenth and nineteenth centuries could not cope with such incongruity. Its affront to stylistic decorum was thought to be on a par with the play's shocking lack of respect for the principle of poetic justice, in which the evil are punished and the good are duly rewarded.

In our time, though, we have become skeptical about easy divisions between good and evil, black and white. We understand the play's rapid dissolution of the opposition between insiders and outsiders, "civilized" Romans and "barbaric" Goths. And we also understand the juxtaposition of radically differing styles. Modern movies have made us familiar with characters like Aaron the Moor, who delivers a verbal pun one moment and a stab in the guts the next. Titus' unexpected laugh helps us to comprehend the way in which human beings deal with inexpressible anguish, rather as Brian Keenan, one of the Western hostages in Lebanon, describes in his memoir, *An Evil Cradling,* his discovery of the saving grace of humour: "In the most inhuman of circumstances men grow and deepen in humanity. In the face of death but not because of it, they explode with passionate life, conquering despair with insane humour."

Whilst making us face the worst that we humans can do to one another and to ourselves, *Titus* also offers us glimpses of the best. Like King Lear, Titus Andronicus journeys from authority to isolation; his wits begin to turn, but through humility he learns to love. There is even a strange tenderness to the way in which he finally puts his daughter out of her misery.

Precisely because of all its extremities, *Titus* is *the* Shakespeare play for our extreme time,

our millennial moment of dark memory and fresh hope. Whatever the new century may bring in the way of transplant surgery and "virtual reality" experiences, for so long as we are human we will need to go on living with our bodies. *Titus* speaks from the distant past to the waiting future, and says: Whoever you may think you are—general, emperor, child, clown—you are flesh and bone. Your being is spoken by your body.

The body of Titus Andronicus has been battered by years of war, and yet he survives. Shakespeare reminds us that real human beings are not supermen or last action heroes, but vulnerable creatures. Titus is scarred, muddy, physically made to stoop low, yet he remains high and indomitable in spirit, despite all the wrongs he has to endure in a cruel world devoid of divine justice:

> Marcus, we are but shrubs, no cedars we,
> No big-boned men framed of the Cyclops'
>   size;
> But metal, Marcus. Steel to the very back,
> Yet wrung with wrongs more than our
>   backs can bear.

Such lines as these are as taut in expression and noble in sentiment as any that Shakespeare would write.

The movie *Titus* was made at the Cinecittà studios in Rome, and such scenes as Saturninus' imperial orgy inevitably invite comparison with *Fellini Satyricon,* especially since Taymor's production designer, Dante Ferretti, worked with the legendary Italian director. There are also touches of Pier Paolo Pasolini, master of the dramatization of emotional extremity in harshly lit landscapes. But the richest influence is Shakespeare's own proto-cinematic imagination. Taymor has the gift of finding visual equivalents for the dramatist's figurative verse. The two locations at the centre of her *Titus,* a swamp and a crossroads, are peculiarly haunting. They translate Shakespearean poetry into the language of cinema. At the same time, the film fully respects the original words, reproducing a much higher percentage of text than most other recent screen adaptations of Shakespeare.

Like Pasolini, Shakespeare believed that ancient myths may speak to modern times. *Titus Andronicus* mingles mythology, history and invention. The story is patterned on the tale in Ovid's *Metamorphoses* of Philomel, who is raped by her brother-in-law. He cuts out her tongue so that she cannot reveal his identity, but she finds another way of communicating, so enabling her sister to serve up a horrible revenge for dinner. Shakespeare took this mythic prototype and retold it through an invented narrative about a fictional Roman general, Titus Andronicus, who returns from successful wars against the Goths only to find himself at odds with the new emperor. Rome collapses into chaos from within.

The play is set simultaneously in timeless myth, imperial Rome and Shakespeare's own Europe. Taymor, too, creates a stylish interplay of past and present, with chariots one moment and motorcycles the next. She reads *Titus* as a compendium of two thousand years of warfare and violence. The Colosseum scenes were shot in Croatia—proximity to Bosnia and Kosovo was a constant reminder that the atrocities of war are always with us.

Titus is not so much a historical work as a meditation on history. We might call it a "meta-history." The political structures of the early Roman republic and the decadence of the late Roman Empire are deliberately overlaid upon each other. They are also mingled with the pre-occupations of late-Elizabethan England: the opening political dispute between Saturninus and Bassianus is over the question of the succession of the recently deceased emperor, a matter of considerable concern at the time Shakespeare was writing, when the old Virgin

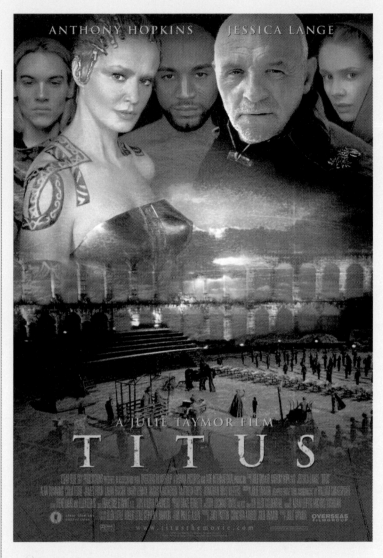

Movie poster for the European release of Julie Taymor's Titus.

Queen was nearing the end of her life and there were several rival candidates to succeed her.

We are asked to imagine that this could be any time in the Roman era and no time. The spiral of revenge begins with an act of human sacrifice (the slaying of Tamora's son Alarbus to appease the shades of those of Titus' sons who have been killed in the wars against the Goths). Historically, human sacrifice was never practiced in ancient Rome, but all cultures have their foundational myths of sacrifice. For Shakespeare and his audience, Rome was evocative of the Roman Catholic church as well as the pagan empire of the past. So it is that the action is suffused with hints of that ultimate sacrifice, the crucifixion of God's own Son. The word *martyr'd* is applied to Lavinia, and when she assists her father in the butchery of Chiron and Demetrius, she is asked to "receive [the] blood," a phrase that darkly parodies the language of the Eucharist, in which we are redeemed by the symbolic blood of Christ. The visionary sequence at the turning point of the movie, where a sacrificial lamb mutates into a myriad of angels, might be seen as Taymor's distinctive response to the play's half-hidden blending of the classical and the Judeo-Christian.

The power and complexity of the sacrifice motif gives the movie an almost primal force. But the treatment of violence is as modern—as postmodern, indeed—as it is ancient. *Titus,* says Taymor, is "about how we make entertainment out of violence." Hence the opening sequence, adapted from the director's 1994 New York stage production of the play, in which a boy stages a battle of toy soldiers to the accompaniment of TV violence. Play becomes reality as war intrudes and the child is catapulted into the ancient Colosseum. The subsequent action is witnessed through his eyes—which become our eyes.

The presence of pity in the act of witnessing is one reason why, for all its horrors, *Titus* is no horror movie. Both the characters and the audience go on an inward journey in which the human *reaction* to violence is of more consequence than the violence itself. At the heart of the movie is a scene involving the killing of a fly in which black comedy momentarily gives way to an exquisite tenderness, delicately rendered by both Taymor's camera and Anthony Hopkins' performance as Titus.

Only a great actor at the height of his powers can do justice to the sheer range of feeling within the character of Titus Andronicus. Laurence Olivier achieved it in Peter Brook's groundbreaking 1955 Stratford-upon-Avon stage production, which redeemed the play from centuries of neglect and disparagement. Now Hopkins, who began his career under Olivier in the early days of London's National Theatre, has achieved it on film. His performance is not without moments of homage to Olivier's grand style, but it is richest when it is quiet rather than loud, especially when the once proud general is reduced to seeking tearful sympathy from the stones in the roadway. Titus' outburst against the injustice of the world is equally memorable: "If there were reason for these miseries, / Then into limits could I bind my woes."

As Titus anticipates Lear, so his opponent, Tamora, queen of the Goths (Jessica Lange), is a glorious combination of Lady Macbeth and Cleopatra. We understand her motives from the start: she is simultaneously a proud queen who has been humiliated and a loving mother whose eldest son has been ripped from her. Shakespeare's text compares her to a "ravenous tiger," an image Taymor brings to the screen in one of the film's surreal dreamlike insets. Tamora is fierce because she is protective of her young—a Tiger Queen, out for revenge against Titus because he has ordered the sacrificial execution of Alarbus.

Her two younger sons, Chiron and Demetrius, are disturbingly familiar to an early-twenty-first-century audience. Bored young Goths, they go on a killing spree for the sheer hell of it. The movie had wrapped before the massacre at Columbine High School in Colorado, but Taymor sensed the resonance when it happened. Yet Shakespeare doesn't crudely demonize these boys. He shows us that it is peer group pressure and the spirit of competition that lead young men to kill and rape.

Tamora's boys are egged on by her lover, Aaron the Moor (compellingly played by Harry Lennix, the one actor in the movie retained from Taymor's stage version). Aaron is the first great Shakespearean villain, the forerunner of Richard III, Iago and Edmund in *King Lear*. But he is also the first great black role in English drama. Taymor regards the part as more complex than that of Othello. Aaron is motivated throughout by his status as an outsider. At first, he seems to be the devil incarnate. But towards the end, there is an astonishing turnaround. "Zounds, ye whore!" he says to the nurse who hands him his first-born son with an insult; "Is black so base a hue?" Black pride and paternal affection undo the ancient racist equation of darkness with evil.

Shakespeare's text is not explicit about the final fate of Aaron's baby. His survival will depend on the integrity of Lucius, Titus' only surviving son. Will the cycle of blood for blood go on, or is there hope for the future? Taymor's stage production was ambiguous, whereas the movie ends on an uplifting note with a closing image of singular beauty, evoking a new dawn. This might seem untrue to Shakespeare's text, which ends with the meting out of punishment to Aaron and Tamora. And yet in a deeper sense the feeling of release is also in the text: after all the cruelty, the word that rings in our ears at the close is "pity."

Through her combination of fidelity and invention, Julie Taymor has made a movie of rare integrity. In a Hollywood ruled by compromise and artistic corner-cutting, she has fully respected both an ancient work of art and a modern company of screen actors. Her reward is to have created something very special. Where so many movies impress at the time but fade in the instant you walk out of the theatre, *Titus* keeps on growing in the imagination.

—Jonathan Bate

Widely regarded as one of the world's leading Shakespearean scholars, JONATHAN BATE is the author of *Shakespeare and Ovid,* the definitive Arden edition of *Titus Andronicus* and *The Genius of Shakespeare.* He is King Alfred Professor of English Literature and Leverhulme Research Professor at the University of Liverpool in England.

Concept drawing by Dante Ferretti.

TITUS
Anthony Hopkins

AARON
Harry Lennix

Rome is but a

CHIRON
Jonathan Rhys Meyers

MARCUS
Colm Feore

DEMETRIUS
Matthew Rhys

SATURNINUS
Alan Cumming

TAMORA
Jessica Lange

wilderness of
tigers

LUCIUS
Angus Macfadyen

BASSIANUS
James Frain

LAVINIA
Laura Fraser

YOUNG LUCIUS
Osheen Jones

TITUS

THE ILLUSTRATED SCREENPLAY

THE PLAYERS

YOUNG LUCIUS, a boy, son of Lucius

TITUS ANDRONICUS, Roman general,
    victorious over the Goths

MARCUS ANDRONICUS, his brother,
    a tribune

LUCIUS
QUINTUS
MARTIUS } his sons
MUTIUS

LAVINIA, his daughter

TAMORA, Queen of the Goths,
    afterwards Empress of Rome

ALARBUS
DEMETRIUS } her sons
CHIRON

AARON, a Moor, her lover

SATURNINUS, son of the late Emperor
    of Rome, afterwards Emperor

BASSIANUS, his younger brother

AEMILIUS, a Roman politician

PUBLIUS, son of Marcus

SEMPRONIUS
CAIUS } Titus' kinsmen
VALENTINE

NURSE

CLOWN

Senators, Tribunes, Roman Soldiers,
    Attendants, other Romans, Goths

INT. KITCHEN OF AN URBAN APARTMENT — NIGHT

We could be in Brooklyn or Sarajevo.

A young boy of ten, **YOUNG LUCIUS**, eats his supper alone at the kitchen table. He wears a brown paper bag over his head with primitive holes cut out for his eyes and mouth. His bag head is illuminated by the glow of an unseen television set. Toy soldiers in war formation litter the table: plastic Romans, G.I. Joes, Superheroes, ketchup and mustard bottles.

A musical-sound montage, seeming to emanate from the TV, begins innocently with the voices of Popeye, the Three Stooges, TV and radio heroes, etc.—cartoon violence that entertains **YOUNG LUCIUS** as he begins to play with his food, stabbing one soldier with a fork or grabbing two others and enacting a mock battle between them.

In the next thirty seconds the sounds of violence will escalate in madness to include cavalry calls, sirens, machine gun fire, marching armies, airplanes, bomb explosions, etc. The sounds propel **YOUNG LUCIUS** into a kinetic frenzy, jumping up and down on his chair, stabbing and slicing at his meat, his toys, raining salt storms from the shaker as he creates a ravaged battlefield of the table, dousing his wounded soldiers in ketchup blood. The horror. The fun.

No longer the canned sound of the TV, the noise has become deafening and palpably real. **YOUNG LUCIUS'** hands shoot up to cover his ears, the sound too real. An explosion rattles the room, as glasses and plates shatter to the floor.

The kitchen has caught on fire. **YOUNG LUCIUS**, terrified, scrambles under the table, still clutching his hands to his ears as the sounds of war overwhelm him.

Out of nowhere the thick hands of **THE CLOWN** grab **YOUNG LUCIUS**, drag him out from under the table and rip the bag off of the child's head to reveal tears streaming down his frightened face.

INT. STAIRS OF THE APARTMENT HOUSE — NIGHT

In an instant this obese and grotesque apparition, **THE CLOWN**, wearing goggles, a World War I leather helmet, baggy pants, a soiled undershirt and suspenders, is running down the stairs of the apartment house, **YOUNG LUCIUS** held tight in his arms. As they burst through the door there is a huge blast and darkness.

The smoky blackness gives way to light as the two exit the apartment building and find themselves in . . .

EXT. INSIDE THE ROMAN COLOSSEUM — NIGHT

NOTE: *All of the buildings in the film are present-day ruins of the ancient Roman empire. Time is blended. In costume as well. It is simultaneously ancient Rome and the second half of the twentieth century.*

The sound of a cheering crowd hails **THE CLOWN** as he holds the saved **YOUNG LUCIUS** high over his head like a trophy, smack in the middle of the arena. **YOUNG LUCIUS**, stunned, looks about him to see the colosseum bleachers empty. Once placed on the ground he turns around to see the ruins of his apartment building, a facade only, burning. A fanfare of thunderous drums draws his attention to the far end of the colosseum.

TITLES BEGIN

Drums and trumpets hail the entry into the arena of hundreds of soldiers returning from war. It is a surreal sight as these figures ceremoniously move towards **YOUNG LUCIUS**. Their armour and visible skin are cracked and black as soot as if emerging from an inferno. In the lead are **MARTIUS**, **MUTIUS**, **QUINTUS** and **LUCIUS** (father of **YOUNG LUCIUS**), **TITUS' SONS**. After them march a series of soldiers bearing dead bodies on stretchers. The great general **TITUS ANDRONICUS** appears on his blackened chariot followed by a cart bearing the captured enemy Goth queen, **TAMORA**, and her sons, **ALARBUS**, **DEMETRIUS** and **CHIRON**. Wearing muddied, long fur coats, they are manacled and chained together. **AARON** the Moor follows, chained to the cart, his bare feet bleeding from the long march.

The parade comes to a halt. The stretchers are set down in the middle of the field and the soldiers stand in formation, their right arms, which appear as swords, held in vertical position. For a moment there is stillness and silence. In unison the soldiers burst into a display of violent martial movement, lasting only ten seconds, then stillness again. The crowd roars. To the heroic notes of a trumpet fanfare the **SOLDIERS** solemnly remove their helmets and look up to acknowledge the invisible cheering crowd.

TITUS removes his helmet and hands it to **YOUNG LUCIUS**, who regards his grandfather with awe and respect. Though exhaustion from years at war is seared into his face, he summons up energy to salute and address the people of Rome.

TITLES END

Hail,
Rome,
Victorious in thy
mourning weeds!

TITUS
Hail, Rome, victorious in thy mourning weeds!
Lo, as the bark that hath discharged her fraught
Returns with precious lading to the bay
From whence at first she weigh'd her anchorage,
Cometh Andronicus, bound with laurel-boughs,
To re-salute his country with his tears.
Stand gracious to the rights that we intend!
Romans, of five-and-twenty valiant sons,
Behold the poor remains, alive and dead!
These that survive let Rome reward with love;
These that I bring unto their latest home,
With burial amongst their ancestors:
Here Goths have given me leave to sheathe my sword.

> **TITUS** sheathes his sword. For a second he falters as if from a skipped heartbeat or loss of wind. **YOUNG LUCIUS**, concerned, touches his grandfather **TITUS'** shoulder gently. **TITUS** continues to talk, but to himself.

TITUS (*cont'd*)
Titus, unkind, and careless of thine own,
Why suffer'st thou thy sons, unburied yet,
To hover on the dreadful shore of Styx?
(*to the Soldiers*)
Make way to lay them by their brethren.

INT. THE ROMAN BATHS — DAY

> The **SONS** of **TITUS** and other **SOLDIERS**, some with missing limbs and war wounds, bathe in the communal baths. The mud streams down their naked bodies as they purify themselves for the burial rites of their brothers.

INT./EXT. THE STEPS OF THE TOMB

> A funeral procession heralded by drums and trumpets descends into the corridors of the tomb. **TITUS** leads his family, soldiers bearing the dead. **TAMORA, DEMETRIUS, CHIRON, ALARBUS** and **AARON** are in attendance.

INT. CORRIDORS INTO THE CATACOMBS OF THE TOMB — DAY

> The procession moves through the corridors . . .

EXT. THE IRON GATES OF THE MAUSOLEUM — DAY

> **YOUNG LUCIUS** follows the **FAMILY** and **SOLDIERS** carrying the dead into the tomb . . .

Here Goths have given me leave to sheathe my sword.

INT. THE ANDRONICUS FAMILY MAUSOLEUM — DAY

> The catacomb is lit by torches. The procession enters the tomb. **TAMORA** and company are left outside the gate, guarded.

TITUS
O sacred receptacle of my joys,
Sweet cell of virtue and nobility,
How many sons of mine hast thou in store,
That thou wilt never render to me more!

> **TITUS** kneels before a bier and undrapes a blanket exposing eight standing pairs of worn and muddy army boots. He scoops up a handful of sand from the ritual container and ceremoniously fills the boots with sand. His living **SONS** and **YOUNG LUCIUS** bow their heads.

TITUS (*cont'd*)
There greet in silence, as the dead are wont,
And sleep in peace, slain in your country's wars!

> There is an awkward moment of silence as **TITUS** drifts away in reverie. The presiding **PRIEST** looks to the **SONS**. Impatient, **LUCIUS**, the eldest son, steps towards his father and in a commanding voice continues with the appropriate rites. As he speaks, **TWO GUARDS** bring in the chained **TAMORA** and her **SONS**.

LUCIUS
Give us the proudest prisoner of the Goths,
That we may hew his limbs, and on a pile
'Ad manes fratrum' sacrifice his flesh,
That so the shadows be not unappeased,
Nor we disturb'd with prodigies on earth.

> **TITUS**, back to the business at hand, rises and dispassionately points to **ALARBUS**, standing with his mother and brothers.

TITUS
I give him you,—the noblest that survives,
The eldest son of this distressed queen.

> **MARTIUS** and **QUINTUS** grab a resistant **ALARBUS** and drag him to the altar. **LUCIUS** and **MUTIUS** go to the altar and begin to purify the swords in the flames.

> **TAMORA** interrupts the ceremony.

TAMORA
Stay, Roman brethren!—Gracious conqueror,
Victorious Titus, rue the tears I shed,
A mother's tears in passion for her son:

Away with him! and make a fire straight; And with our swords, upon a pile of wood, Let's hew his limbs till they be clean consumed.

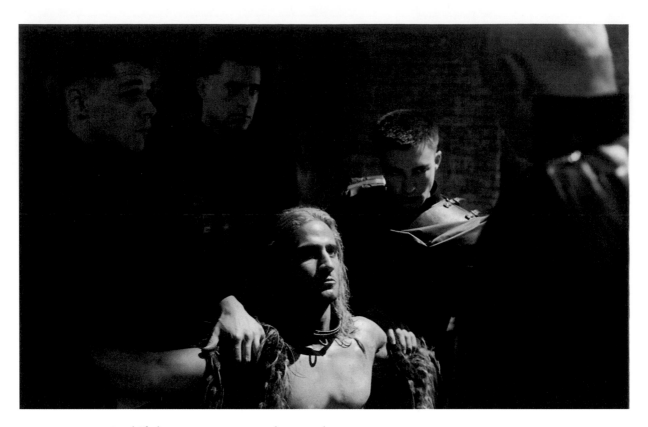

And if thy sons were ever dear to thee,
O, think my son to be as dear to me!

> For a moment the SONS halt the routine and look to TITUS for
> instruction. TITUS does not look at TAMORA but listens.

TAMORA (*cont'd*)
Sufficeth not, that we are brought to Rome,
To beautify thy triumphs and return,
Captive to thee and thy Roman yoke;
But must my sons be slaughter'd in the streets,
For valiant doings in their country's cause?
O, if to fight for king and commonweal
Were piety in thine, it is in these.

> TITUS, unmoved, nods for the ceremony to go on. TAMORA,
> shocked that TITUS does not comply and identify with her reason-
> ing, changes tact and begins to plead. ALARABUS' clothes are ripped
> off and he is forced to drink from the goblet, wine spilling down his
> naked chest. TAMORA falls to her knees in desperation.

TAMORA (*cont'd*)
Andronicus, stain not thy tomb with blood:
Wilt thou draw near the nature of the gods?
Draw near them, then, in being merciful:
Sweet mercy is nobility's true badge:
Thrice-noble Titus, spare my first-born son.

> TITUS has moved to the altar and picks up the dagger.

TITUS
Patient yourself, madam, and pardon me.
These are their brethren, whom your Goths beheld

Alive and dead; and for their brethren slain
Religiously they ask a sacrifice.

> He goes to **ALARBUS** and, with coolness, slices a line across his chest with the dagger, drawing blood. This is routine ritual for him.

TITUS (*cont'd*)
To this your son is mark'd; and die he must,
T'appease their groaning shadows that are gone.

LUCIUS
Away with him! and make a fire straight;
And with our swords, upon a pile of wood,
Let's hew his limbs till they be clean consumed.

> The **SONS** of **TITUS** take **ALARBUS** and exit the mausoleum.

> **TAMORA** and her two sons huddle together observing **TITUS** cleanse the ritual dagger. **YOUNG LUCIUS** watches his grandfather's every move.

TAMORA
O cruel, irreligious piety!

CHIRON
Was ever Scythia half so barbarous!

DEMETRIUS
Oppose not Scythia to ambitious Rome.
Alarbus goes to rest; and we survive
To tremble under Titus' threatening looks.
Stand resolved; but hope withal,
The gods may favour Tamora, the Queen of Goths,
To quit these bloody wrongs upon her foes.

> The **SONS** of **TITUS** return from the raging bonfires, marching in formation to the altar with their swords bloody and their foreheads smeared with ritual blood. **LUCIUS** throws the entrails of **ALARBUS** into the sacrificial bowl of fire on the altar.

LUCIUS
See, lord and father, how we have perform'd
Our Roman rites: Alarbus' limbs are lopp'd,
And entrails feed the sacrificing fire,
Remaineth naught, but to inter our brethren,
And with loud 'larums welcome them to Rome.

> Montage: **TITUS** and **TAMORA** face each other, the ritual fire between them. Scores of dead warriors are laid to rest. Their embalmed bodies placed in the walls of the mass crypt. **YOUNG LUCIUS** and **TITUS** light candles for the dead.

Lo, at this tomb my tributary tears
I render, for my brethren's
obsequies; And at thy feet I kneel,
with tears of joy, Shed on the
earth, for thy return to Rome

TITUS

In peace and honour rest you here, my sons;
Secure from worldly chances and mishaps!
Here lurks no treason, here no envy swells,
Here grow no damned drugs, here are no storms,
No noise, but silence and eternal sleep.

> LAVINIA, TITUS' daughter, enters the mausoleum. Framed
> in a shadowed archway, she silently watches her father. She
> is a young woman of incredible beauty, which we glean
> through her mourning veil.

TITUS (*cont'd*)

In peace and honour rest you here, my sons!

> LAVINIA goes to TITUS, kneels and raises her veil. She opens
> a vial of tears and sprinkles them in a circle before the altar.

LAVINIA

In peace and honour live Lord Titus long;
My noble lord and father, live in fame!
Lo, at this tomb my tributary tears
I render, for my brethren's obsequies;
And at thy feet I kneel, with tears of joy,
Shed on the earth, for thy return to Rome:
O, bless me here with thy victorious hand.

TITUS

Kind Rome, that hast thus lovingly reserved
The cordial of mine age to glad my heart!
Lavinia, live; outlive thy father's days,
And fame's eternal date, for virtue's praise!

**EXT. A PUBLIC SQUARE BEFORE THE STEPS
OF THE CAPITOL — DAY**

> YOUNG LUCIUS sits alone on the vast steps of the Capitol
> Building. The square is empty. Black silk banners tumble
> from the myriad of arched balconies of the Capitol
> Building behind him. A breeze blows a sheet of newspaper
> by YOUNG LUCIUS. He runs to catch it. For a second he
> glances at the headlines:

> THE ROMAN TIMES
>
> THOUSANDS MOURN THE DEATH OF CAESAR
>
> GENERAL TITUS ANDRONICUS RETURNS
> VICTORIOUS TO ROME
>
> ELECTIONS HELD IN THE SENATE TODAY

As he begins to fold the news into a paper airplane the sound of a distant loudspeaker and rallying mob seize his attention.

EXT. STREET OF ROME — DAY

YOUNG LUCIUS runs into a narrow street and is practically run over by soldiers on horseback leading a motorcade. Standing in a bulletproof, glass-covered '30s convertible is SATURNINUS, the late emperor's eldest son. The loudspeaker mounted on the car blasts his speech through the narrow streets. Behind the car marches a volatile band of SATURNINUS' FOLLOWERS. YOUNG LUCIUS is swept along in the excitement.

SATURNINUS
Noble patricians, patrons of my right,
Defend the justice of my cause with arms;
And, countrymen, my loving followers,
Plead my successive title with your swords.

EXT. ANOTHER STREET OF ROME — DAY

Another motorcade in progress. BASSIANUS, SATURNINUS' younger brother, standing in an open '50s convertible car, campaigning over the loudspeaker. [BASSIANUS' and SATURNINUS' speeches overlap. The scene is intercut as the two parties weave their way through the streets of Rome and finally confront each other in the large open square in front of the Capitol.]

BASSIANUS
Romans, friends, followers, favourers of my right,
If ever Bassianus, Caesar's son,
Were gracious in the eyes of royal Rome,
Keep, then, this passage to the Capitol.

EXT. ANOTHER STREET OF ROME — DAY

SATURNINUS
I am the first-born son, that was the last
That ware the imperial diadem of Rome.

EXT. ANOTHER STREET OF ROME — DAY

BASSIANUS
And suffer not dishonour to approach
The imperial seat, to virtue consecrate,
To justice, continence, and nobility.

EXT. A PUBLIC SQUARE BEFORE THE STEPS OF THE CAPITOL — DAY

The two motorcades confront each other as they enter the crowded Public Square.

SATURNINUS
Then let my father's honours live in me,
Nor wrong mine age with this indignity.

BASSIANUS
But let desert in pure election shine;
And, Romans, fight for freedom in your choice.

During the speeches MARCUS ANDRONICUS, a tribune and brother to TITUS, appears on the balcony of the Capitol. He observes the rival SONS of the late emperor. At his side stands AEMILIUS, an older tribune holding a crown, and PUBLIUS, a younger tribune carrying white robes.

The Capitol's arched balconies fill with TRIBUNES.

A conflict erupts between the TWO BROTHERS and among their followers. MARCUS, AEMILIUS and PUBLIUS leave the balcony and reappear through the large doors at the top of the Capitol steps. The fracas subsides.

Open the gates and let me in.

MARCUS
Princes,—that strive by factions and by friends
Ambitiously for rule and empery,
Know that the people of Rome have, by common voice,
In election for the Roman empery,
Chosen Andronicus,
A nobler man, a braver warrior,
Lives not this day within the city walls:
He by the senate is accited home
From weary wars against the barbarous Goths;
Let us entreat, by honour of his name,
That you withdraw you,
Dismiss your followers, and, as suitors should,
Plead your deserts in peace and humbleness.

> A low grumble from the crowds is hushed by
> BASSIANUS.

BASSIANUS
Marcus Andronicus, so I do rely
On thy uprightness and integrity,
And so I love and honour thee and thine,
Thy noble brother Titus and his sons,
And her to whom my thoughts are humbled all,
Gracious Lavinia, Rome's rich ornament,
That I will here dismiss my loving friends;
And to my fortunes and the people's favour
Commit my cause in balance to be weigh'd.

> He signals to his followers to back off and then mounts the steps to
> take the white robe from PUBLIUS, signifying that he is a candidate
> for election as emperor. There is a tense pause as everyone waits for
> SATURNINUS to reply. Smugly he laughs at his
> brother and then turns to address his followers.

SATURNINUS
Friends, that have been thus forward in my right,
I thank you all, and here dismiss you all;

> He mounts the steps to take the white robe.

SATURNINUS (*cont'd*)
And to the love and favour of my country
Commit myself, my person, and the cause.
Rome, be as just and gracious unto me
As I am confident and kind to thee.
Open the gates and let me in.

SATURNINUS moves towards the entryway to the Senate, followed by BASSIANUS and the TRIBUNES.

MARCUS waits on the steps, searching the dispersing crowds for signs of TITUS. Noise from the crowd signals that he is approaching with his SONS and LAVINIA. The crowds part to let TITUS' chariot through. TITUS dismounts and approaches his brother. Their embrace is both formal and passionate.

YOUNG LUCIUS sees his father and runs to his side.

MARCUS
Long live Lord Titus, my beloved brother.

TITUS
Thanks, gentle tribune, noble brother Marcus.

SATURNINUS and BASSIANUS reappear in the doorway.

MARCUS
And welcome, nephews, from successful wars,
You that survive and those that sleep in fame.

BASSIANUS spots LAVINIA and goes to her. They shyly kiss, which does not go unnoticed by TITUS. MARCUS mounts the steps and nods to PUBLIUS who brings a white robe to TITUS.

MARCUS (*cont'd*)
Titus Andronicus, the people of Rome
Send thee by me, their tribune and their trust,
This palliament of white and spotless hue;
And name thee in election for the empire,
With these our late-deceased emperor's sons:
Be 'candidatus,' then, and put it on,
And help to set a head on headless Rome.

TITUS
A better head her glorious body fits
Than his that shakes for age and feebleness:

He turns to address the people.

TITUS (*cont'd*)
Rome, I have been thy soldier forty years,
And led my country's strength successfully,
And buried one-and-twenty valiant sons,
Give me a staff of honour for mine age,
But not a sceptre to control the world:
Upright he held it, lords, that held it last.

He turns to give back the robe to MARCUS.

MARCUS (*under his breath*)
Titus, thou shalt but ask and have the empery.

SATURNINUS
(*having overheard, he steps forward, sarcastically challenging*)
Proud and ambitious tribune, canst thou tell?

TITUS
Patience, Prince Saturnine.

SATURNINUS (*angry*)
Romans, do me right;

>   He throws the white robe to the ground.

SATURNINUS (*cont'd*)
Patricians, draw your swords, and sheathe them not
Till Saturninus be Rome's emperor.
Andronicus, would thou wert shipp'd to hell,
Rather than rob me of the people's hearts!

>   LUCIUS strides forward to confront SATURNINUS, his hand on the
>   hilt of his sword, ready.

LUCIUS
Proud Saturnine, interrupter of the good
That noble-minded Titus means to thee!

A better head her glorious body fits... Than his that shakes for age and feebleness...

TITUS instantly comes between them, deferring to a fuming SA-TURNINUS.

TITUS
Content thee, prince; I will restore to thee
The people's hearts, and wean them from themselves.

SATURNINUS turns his back on TITUS and moves down the steps to his followers. The air is thick with tension as hands go to sword hilts and a sea of mumbling rises in pitch. TITUS watches SATURNINUS carefully as BASSIANUS steals up behind TITUS to whisper in his ear.

BASSIANUS
Andronicus, I do not flatter thee,
But honour thee, and will do till I die:
My faction if thou strengthen with thy friends,
I will most thankful be.

TITUS does not pay attention to BASSIANUS but is still focused on SATURNINUS.

TITUS
People of Rome, and people's tribunes here,
I ask your voices and your suffrages:
Will you bestow them friendly on Andronicus?

At the top of the steps the TRIBUNES confer with one another. AEMELIUS speaks for all.

AEMELIUS
To gratify the good Andronicus,
And gratulate his safe return to Rome,
The people will accept whom he admits.

TITUS
Tribunes, I thank you: and this suit I make,
That you create your emperor's eldest son,
Lord Saturnine; whose virtues will, I hope,
Reflect on Rome as Titan's rays on earth,
And if you will elect by my advice,
Crown him, and say, "Long live our emperor!"

For a moment there is a stony silence. TITUS' SONS gather together while BASSIANUS retreats to LAVINIA in shock. SATURNINUS' followers take the lead and then the rest of the crowd joins in.

AEMILIUS
Long live our emperor, Saturnine!

They kneel. A stunned but definitely pleased SATURNINUS mounts the steps to receive the crown. He smiles on TITUS as he passes him.

MARCUS (*hiding his dismay*)
Patricians and plebeians, we create
Lord Saturninus Rome's great emperor,
And say, "Long live our Emperor Saturnine!"

A gold laurel-wreath crown is placed on SATURNINUS' head.

INT. THE SENATE — LATER THAT AFTERNOON

SATURNINUS sits on the throne. The TRIBUNES, MARCUS, TITUS and his FAMILY are in attendance. BASSIANUS stands with LAVINIA. Though the air is solemn SATURNINUS is enjoying himself and his new power.

SATURNINUS
Titus Andronicus, for thy favours done
To us in our election this day
I give thee thanks in part of thy deserts,
And will with deeds requite thy gentleness:
And, for an onset, Titus, to advance
Thy name and honourable family,
Lavinia will I make my empress,
Rome's royal mistress, mistress of my heart,
And in the sacred Pantheon her espouse:
Tell me, Andronicus, doth this motion please thee?

TITUS is on the spot. LAVINIA looks to a disgusted and furious BASSIANUS and then to her father with pleading fear. TITUS' SONS are also in a state of shock knowing that their sister is engaged to BASSIANUS. TITUS looks away from his daughter, giving his answer quickly and humbly.

TITUS
It doth, my worthy lord; and in this match
I hold me highly honour'd of your Grace.

> He guides LAVINIA to the throne, her head bowed. An obedient
> daughter, she ascends the throne and kisses SATURNINUS' hand.
> SATURNINUS smiles at his new prize. He knows she detests him.

> BASSIANUS storms out of the Senate and nearly collides into the
> prisoners, TAMORA, her SONS and AARON, who have been brought
> in as gifts to the new emperor.

TITUS (*cont'd*)
And here, in sight of Rome, to Saturnine
King and commander of our commonweal,
The wide world's emperor—do I consecrate
My sword, my chariot, and my prisoners;
Presents well worthy Rome's imperial lord.

> TITUS hands over his sword and the gold reins, representing his
> chariot, to a GUARD, as the PRISONERS are forced to kneel at the
> base of the throne.

SATURNINUS
Thanks, noble Titus, father of my life!
How proud I am of thee and of thy gifts
Rome shall record; and when I do forget
The least of these unspeakable deserts,
Romans, forget thy fealty to me.

TITUS (*to Tamora*)
Now, madam, are you prisoner to an emperor;
To him that, for your honour and your state,
Will use you nobly and your followers.

TAMORA looks up at TITUS with venom in her eyes and then away. Meanwhile, SATURNINUS descends from his throne to have a good look at his booty.

SATURNINUS
A goodly lady, trust me; of the hue
That I would choose, were I to choose anew.

He gently puts his hand under TAMORA's chin and lifts her face to look into her eyes. As he speaks her expression transforms from one of defiance to one of subtle sexuality. Instantly she knows she has an ally. SATURNINUS could be clay in TAMORA's hands.

SATURNINUS (*cont'd*)
Clear up, fair queen, that cloudy countenance:
Though chance of war hath wrought this change of cheer,
Thou comest not to be made a scorn in Rome:
Princely shall be thy usage every way.
Rest on my word, and let not discontent
Daunt all your hopes: madam, he that comforts you
Can make you greater than Queen of Goths.

He realizes that everyone is watching him and that he has gotten a little carried away with TAMORA.

SATURNINUS (*cont'd*)
Lavinia, you are not displeased with this?

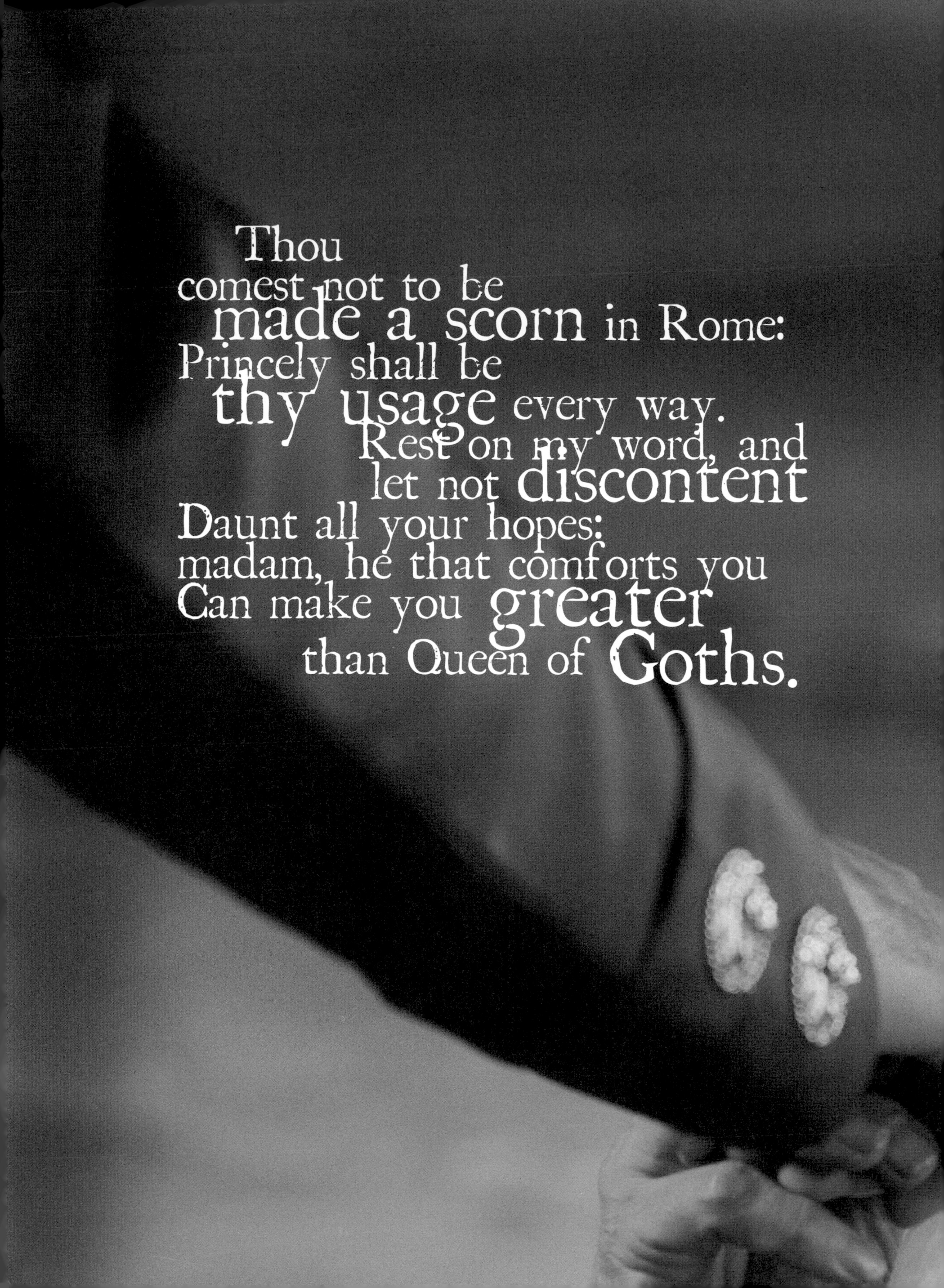

Thou
comest not to be
    made a scorn in Rome:
Princely shall be
    thy usage every way.
            Rest on my word, and
        let not discontent
Daunt all your hopes:
madam, he that comforts you
Can make you greater
        than Queen of Goths.

Lord Titus, by your leave, this maid is mine.

LAVINIA
Not I, my lord; sith true nobility
Warrants these words in princely courtesy.

SATURNINUS
Thanks, sweet Lavinia.—Romans, let us go:
Ransomless here we set our prisoners free:
Proclaim our honours, lords, with trump and drum.

> Again SATURNINUS has shocked everyone with this cavalier pronouncement. Is he mad? TAMORA quickly kisses his hand and SATURNINUS begins to oversee the release of the prisoners.

> TITUS' SONS look to their father for an explanation that he doesn't have.

> TITUS exits from the Senate with LAVINIA followed by the SONS and MARCUS.

EXT. THE SENATE — LATE AFTERNOON

> As TITUS and the others exit the Senate door, BASSIANUS appears and seizes LAVINIA.

BASSIANUS
Lord Titus, by your leave, this maid is mine.

TITUS
How, sir! are you in earnest, then, my lord?

BASSIANUS
Ay, noble Titus; and resolved withal.

MARCUS
This prince in justice seizeth but his own.

> LUCIUS comes between TITUS and BASSIANUS, clearly ready to defend him against his father's will.

LUCIUS
And that he will, and shall, if Lucius live.

> MUTIUS, MARTIUS and QUINTUS, the rest of the SONS, move to stand beside LUCIUS, creating a wall between TITUS and BASSIANUS and LAVINIA. It clearly upsets them to defy their father but they are ready to do so.

> YOUNG LUCIUS watches the rest of the scene from behind a pillar.

TITUS
Traitors, avaunt! Where is the emperor's guard?

> SATURNINUS appears in the doorway.

TITUS (*cont'd*)
Treason, my lord, Lavinia is surprised!

SATURNINUS
Surprised! by whom?

BASSIANUS
By him that justly may
Bear his betrothed from all the world away.

TITUS
Fear not, my lord, and I'll soon bring her back.

> BASSIANUS, MARCUS with LAVINIA flee down a narrow passage-way.
>
> The BROTHERS have drawn their swords defensively. TITUS looks about for support but there are no guards. SATURNINUS has stopped them at the door.
>
> SATURNINUS disappears back into the Senate and the doors close.

EXT. A LONG COLONNADE — LATE AFTERNOON

> MUTIUS, LUCIUS, QUINTUS and MARTIUS follow BASSIANUS and LAVINIA. They veer to the left and continue . . . down the arched corridor of the Capitol Building.

EXT. THE ARCHED CORRIDOR OF THE CAPITOL BUILDING — LATE AFTERNOON

> MUTIUS stops following the BROTHERS at the end of the corridor which opens onto the Capitol steps . . .

MUTIUS
Brothers, help to convey her hence away,
And with my sword I'll keep this way safe.

> TITUS appears and tries to pursue the others, who are now running across the Capitol Square, but is blocked by MUTIUS.

MUTIUS (*cont'd*)
My lord, you pass not here.

TITUS
What, villain boy!
Barr'st me my way in Rome?

> TITUS goes for his own sword but it is missing. (He had bequeathed it to SATURNINUS in the previous scene.) Out of control with rage he grabs the sword from MUTIUS' hands . . .

MUTIUS
Help, Lucius!

Behold, I choose thee, Tamora, for my bride

EXT. THE STEPS OF THE CAPITOL — CONTINUED . . .

At the top of the steps, TITUS thrusts the sword into his son's side. MUTIUS rolls to the bottom of the steps.

Instantly TITUS knows what he has done. MUTIUS, his young face wide eyed in disbelief, falters backwards and then collapses on the pavement, dead. TITUS stands frozen in a state of shock.

LUCIUS runs into the square and halts at the sight before him. He rushes to MUTIUS' side, in hope, only to find him dead.

LUCIUS
My lord, you are unjust; and, more than so,
In wrongful quarrel you have slain your son.

TITUS
Nor thou, nor he, are any sons of mine;
My sons would never so dishonour me:
Traitor, restore Lavinia to the emperor.

LUCIUS
Dead, if you will; but not to be his wife,
That is another's lawful promised love.

LUCIUS picks up MUTIUS, slings him over his shoulder and hurriedly traverses the square.

YOUNG LUCIUS, who had been hiding up until this time, bolts across the square to follow his father.

TITUS turns towards the Capitol Building and is surprised to be face-to-face with SATURNINUS. TAMORA, DEMETRIUS, CHIRON, AARON and a few of the TRIBUNES have also emerged from the building to observe the proceedings. TITUS starts to speak but is cut off . . .

SATURNINUS
No, Titus, no; the emperor needs her not,
Nor her, nor thee, nor any of thy stock:
I'll trust, by leisure, him that mocks me once;
Thee never, nor thy traitorous haughty sons,
Confederates all thus to dishonour me.
But go thy ways; go,
A valiant son-in-law thou shalt enjoy;
One fit to bandy with thy lawless sons.

SATURNINUS turns his back on TITUS and addresses TAMORA.

SATURNINUS (*cont'd*)
And therefore, lovely Tamora, Queen of Goths,
If thou be pleased with this my sudden choice,

Behold, I choose thee, Tamora, for my bride,
And will create thee empress of Rome.
Speak, Queen of Goths, dost thou applaud my choice?

TAMORA (*kneeling while casting a sidelong glance at Titus*)
If Saturnine advance the Queen of Goths,
She will a handmaid be to his desires,
A loving nurse, a mother to his youth.

SATURNINUS (*taking her hand to help her rise*)
Ascend, fair queen, to the Pantheon. Lords, accompany
Your noble emperor and his lovely bride,
There shall we consummate our spousal rites.

> SATURNINUS turns his back on TITUS and motions for everyone else
> to join him in a procession to the Pantheon.

> TITUS, left alone, watches them ascend the steep steps of the Capitol.

EXT. SMALL CITY STREET — SUNSET

> TITUS begins to wander aimlessly down the empty city streets.

TITUS (V.O.)
Titus, when wert thou wont to walk alone,
Dishonour'd thus, and challenged of wrongs?

INT. CORRIDOR IN FRONT OF ANDRONICUS FAMILY TOMB INSIDE THE
MAUSOLEUM

> TITUS appears around a corner, finds himself in front of his family
> tomb. MARCUS, LUCIUS, QUINTUS and MARTIUS approach TITUS
> carrying MUTIUS' body on a makeshift stretcher. They halt just
> before they reach the gates of the tomb. MARCUS pulls the blanket
> from MUTIUS' face to show TITUS.

Titus, when
wert thou wont
to walk alone,
Dishonour'd thus,
and challenged
of wrongs?

MARCUS
O Titus, see, O, see what thou hast done!
In a bad quarrel slain a virtuous son.

TITUS
No, foolish tribune, no; no son of mine,
Nor thou, nor these, confederates in the deed
That hath dishonour'd all our family.

> LUCIUS, disheartened with his father, decides to ignore him and makes a move to bring the body through the gates.

LUCIUS
But let us give him burial, as becomes;
Give Mutius burial with our bretheren.

TITUS (*blocking them*)
Traitors, away! he rests not in this tomb:
Here none but soldiers and Rome's servitors
Repose in fame; none basely slain in brawls:
Bury him where you can, he comes not here.

MARCUS
My lord, this is impiety in you:
He must be buried with his brethren.

QUINTUS
And shall, or him we will accompany.

TITUS
"And shall"! what villain was it spake that word?

QUINTUS
He that would vouch it in any place but here.

TITUS
What, would you bury him in my despite?

> The SONS rest the stretcher on the ground.

MARCUS
No, noble Titus; but entreat of thee
To pardon Mutius, and to bury him.

TITUS
Marcus, even thou hast struck upon my crest,
And, with these boys, mine honour thou hast wounded.
My foes I do repute you every one;
So, trouble me no more, but get you gone.

> He steps away from the tomb and turns his back on all of them.

MARTIUS
He is not with himself; let us withdraw.

QUINTUS
Not I, till Mutius' bones be buried.

MARTIUS (*kneeling*)
Father, and in that name doth nature speak.

LUCIUS (*kneeling*)
Dear father, soul and substance of us all.

MARCUS (*begins to kneel*)
Renowned Titus, more than half my soul.

TITUS
Rise, Marcus, rise:
The dismall'st day is this that e'er I saw,
To be dishonour'd by my sons in Rome!
Well, bury him, and bury me the next.

EXT. THE PALACE ATRIUM — THAT NIGHT

Champagne corks pop and fly. Liquid flows. Big Band music. A wild wedding celebration is in full throttle. Lanterns, dancing, drunken musicians. **DEMETRIUS** and **CHIRON**, dressed to the nines, are high on everything, bouncing around the periphery of a gigantic mosaic swimming pool. Still the "enemy" at heart, they have a heyday dropping cigarette ashes into champagne glasses, tripping the dancing couples, etc. Bad-boy behavior, but innocent.

TAMORA, gorgeous in a sleek, golden metal '30s gown, dances with **SATURNINUS**, who sports a white tuxedo. He has had too much to drink and is getting gropey and boisterous. She pushes him away

playfully and, slightly tipsy herself, moves through the party crowd as if looking for someone.

She spots **AARON** disappearing through one of the doors.

EXT. THE PALACE BALCONY — NIGHT

The balcony of the Palace is on the second floor and overlooks the city. Long steps connect it to a piazza below. Soldiers guard the steps from below.

AARON is leaning against the balustrade staring down into the piazza. He wears a dark suit.

EXT. THE PIAZZA — NIGHT

TITUS is sitting on a large rock. He is alone except for a stray dog sniffing at garbage.

EXT. THE PALACE BALCONY — NIGHT

TAMORA emerges through the archway and lights up at the sight of **AARON**'s back.

She moves to him and just as she's about to speak he shushes her and with his head gestures for her to look at the figures below.

EXT. THE PALACE ATRIUM — NIGHT

DEMETRIUS and **CHIRON** smirk at a much distressed **SATURNINUS** as he searches for **TAMORA** through the dancing **CROWD**.

EXT. THE PIAZZA — NIGHT

> LAVINIA, hand in hand with BASSIANUS, tentatively approaches TITUS from behind. She delicately puts her hand on his shoulder.

EXT. TOP OF THE PALACE STAIRS — NIGHT

> SATURNINUS appears at the top of the steps.

SATURNINUS
So, Bassianus, you have play'd your prize.

EXT. THE PALACE BALCONY — NIGHT

> TAMORA, sensing the trouble ahead, smiles at AARON and turns to leave.

SATURNINUS (O.S. — *cont'd*)
God give you joy, sir, of your gallant bride!

EXT. THE PIAZZA — NIGHT

BASSIANUS (*clearly disturbed*)
And you of yours, my lord! Say no more,
Nor wish no less; and so, I take my leave.

> He tries to draw a reluctant LAVINIA away but she doesn't want to leave her father. On SATURNINUS' next words he halts.

EXT. THE PALACE STAIRS — NIGHT

SATURNINUS (*champagne glass in hand, stumbling down the stairs*)
Traitor, if Rome have law, or we have power,
Thou and thy faction shall repent this rape.

EXT. THE PIAZZA — NIGHT

BASSIANUS (*snaps around, livid*)
Rape, call you it, my lord, to seize my own,
My true-betrothed love, and now my wife?
But let the laws of Rome determine all;
Meanwhile I am possess'd of that is mine.

> By this time **MARCUS**, the **SONS** of **TITUS** and **YOUNG LUCIUS** have
> arrived in the Piazza.

EXT. THE PALACE STAIRS — NIGHT

SATURNINUS (*continuing to descend the stairs*)
'Tis good, sir: you are very short with us;
But, if we live, we'll be as sharp with you.

EXT. THE PIAZZA — NIGHT

> SATURNINUS descends the last steps into
> the Piazza.

BASSIANUS
My lord, what I have done, as best I may,
Answer I must, and shall do with my life.
This noble gentleman, Lord Titus here,
Is in opinion and in honour wrong'd;
That, in the rescue of Lavinia,
With his own hand did slay his youngest son,
In zeal to you,
Receive him, then, to favour, Saturnine!

TITUS
Prince Bassianus, leave to plead my deeds:
'Tis thou and those that have dishonour'd me.
Rome and the righteous heavens be my judge,
How I have loved and honour'd Saturnine!

> He kneels formally to **SATURNINUS** with head bowed. **BASSIANUS**
> can't believe it. **LAVINIA** tries to calm him.

> **TAMORA** appears on the steps behind **SATURNINUS**.

> By this time some of the party guests, **DEMETRIUS** and **CHIRON** have
> come out on the steps to see what's going on.

TAMORA (*coming forward*)
My worthy lord, if ever Tamora
Were gracious in those princely eyes of thine,
Then hear me speak indifferently for all;
And at my suit, sweet, pardon what is past.

SATURNINUS
What, madam! be dishonour'd openly,
And basely put it up without revenge?

TAMORA
Not so, my lord; the gods of Rome forfend
I should be author to dishonour you!
But on mine honour dare I undertake
For good Lord Titus' innocence in all;
Whose fury not dissembled speaks his griefs:
Then, at my suit, look graciously on him;
Lose not so noble a friend on vain suppose.
    (*to Saturninus*)
My lord, be ruled by me, be won at last;
Dissemble all your griefs and discontents:
You are but newly planted in your throne;
Lest, then, the people, and patricians too,
Upon a just survey, take Titus' part,
And so supplant you for ingratitude,
Yield at entreats; and then let me alone.
    (*an aside direct to the camera*)
I'll find a day to massacre them all,
And raze their faction and their family,
The cruel father and his traitorous sons,
To whom I sued for my dear son's life;
And make them know what 'tis to let a queen
Kneel in the streets and beg for grace in vain.
    (*instantly she breaks away from the
    camera and back into a mood of lightness*)
Come, come, sweet emperor,—come, Andronicus,
Take up this good old man, and cheer the heart
That dies in tempest of thy angry frown.

SATURNINUS (*with reluctance*)
Rise, Titus, rise; my empress hath prevail'd.

TITUS
I thank your majesty, and her, my lord.

TAMORA
And let it be mine honour, good my lord,
That I have reconciled your friends and you.

I'll find a day to massacre them all...

And make them know what 'tis to let a queen Kneel in the streets and beg for grace in vain.

For you, Prince Bassianus, I have pass'd
My word and promise to the emperor,
That you will be more mild and tractable.
And fear not, lords,—and you, Lavinia;
By my advice, all humbled on your knees,
You shall ask pardon of his majesty.

    MARCUS, LAVINIA and the SONS of TITUS kneel reluctantly.

LUCIUS
We do; and vow to heaven, and to his highness,
That what we did was mildly as we might,
Tend'ring our sister's honour and our own.

MARCUS
That, on mine honour, here I do attest.

SATURNINUS (*turning to go back up the steps*)
Away, and talk not; trouble us no more.

TAMORA
Nay, nay, sweet emperor, we must all be friends:
The tribune and his nephews kneel for grace;
I will not be denied. Sweet heart, look back.

SATURNINUS
Marcus, for thy sake and thy brother's here,
And at my lovely Tamora's entreats,
I do remit these young men's heinous faults.
Stand up!
Lavinia, though you left me like a churl,
I found a friend;
Come, if the emperor's court can feast two brides,
You are my guest, Lavinia, and your friends.
This day shall be a love-day, Tamora.

    SATURNINUS turns to climb the stairs.

TITUS
To-morrow, an it please your majesty
To hunt the panther and the hart with me.

EXT. THE PALACE STAIRS — NIGHT

SATURNINUS
Be it so, Titus, and gramercy too.

    All but TAMORA and TITUS follow SATURNINUS back up the stairs
    and into the BALLROOM to continue the party and feasting.

DEMETRIUS and CHIRON intentionally brush up against LAVINIA as she passes them on the stairs.

AARON, hanging back in a far corner of the palace balcony, watches everyone as they mount the steps.

DISSOLVE TO: EXT. THE PIAZZA — NIGHT

PENNY ARCADE NIGHTMARE #1

TAMORA and TITUS remain in the Piazza face to face and frozen.

A surreal sequence of images overtakes the screen between the two profiles. The background Piazza becomes an inferno. Through the flames the torso and limbs of a classical Roman marble sculpture fly towards the camera.

On the chest of the sculpture a bloody line magically appears that is a replica of the line TITUS cut into the chest of ALARBUS, TAMORA'S ELDEST SON. The music is replaced by the sound of human breathing. Suddenly the chest of the statue is visibly breathing, rapidly, faster and faster for just five seconds and then stops. Silence.

EXT. THE PIAZZA — NIGHT

TAMORA and TITUS break out of their frozen positions. TAMORA starts to climb the steps as TITUS watches her from below.

AARON (V.O. — *starts during her climb*)
Now climbeth Tamora Olympus' top,
Safe out of fortune's shot; and sits aloft,

EXT. THE PALACE BALCONY — NIGHT

From AARON's POV, TAMORA continues to mount the steps.

AARON (V.O. — *cont'd*)
Secure of thunder's crack or lightning-flash;
Advanced above pale envy's threat'ning reach.

FADE TO BLACK.

FADE IN:

EXT. THE PALACE BALCONY — DAWN

 AARON leaning over the balustrade, looks to the distant hills as the rising sun appears behind them. Some stars are still visible.

AARON (*cont'd*)
As when the golden sun salutes the morn,
And, having gilt the ocean with his beams,
Gallops the zodiac in his glistering coach,
And overlooks the highest-peering hills.

 AARON turns to speak directly to camera.

AARON (*cont'd*)
So Tamora:
Upon her wit doth earthly honour wait,
And virtue stoops and trembles at her frown.
Then, Aaron, arm thy heart, and fit thy thoughts,
To mount aloft with thy imperial mistress,
And mount her pitch, whom thou in triumph long
Hast prisoner held, fetter'd in amorous chains.

 He breaks away from the camera which follows him as he moves down a narrow walkway around the exterior of the palace. From time to time he turns to address the camera directly.

AARON
Away with slavish weeds and servile thoughts!
I will be bright, and shine in pearl and gold,
To wait upon this new-made empress.
To wait, said I? to wanton with this queen,
This goddess, this Semiramis, this nymph,
This siren, that will charm Rome's Saturnine,
And see his shipwrack and his commonweal's.

 The sound of a distant fight interrupts his speech.

AARON (*cont'd*)
Holla! what storm is this?

EXT. THE PALACE ATRIUM — EARLY MORNING

 AARON, upon hearing the voices of **DEMETRIUS** and **CHIRON** quarreling, hides behind a pillar.

A sulky **CHIRON** stomps around the pool followed by **DEMETRIUS**. Servants, cleaning up after last night's wedding celebration, scurry to leave. One or two remain to clean up the mess.

DEMETRIUS
Chiron, thy years wants wit, thy wit wants edge,
And manners, to intrude where I am graced;
And may, for aught thou know'st, affected be.

He pours a flagon of water over his head to cool himself off. As **CHIRON** protests, **DEMETRIUS** teases him by throwing leftovers at him.

CHIRON
Demetrius, thou dost over-ween in all;
And so in this, to bear me down with braves.
'Tis not the difference of a year or two
Makes me less gracious, or thee more fortunate:
I am as able and as fit as thou
To serve, and to deserve my mistress' grace;
And that my sword upon thee shall approve,
And plead my passions for Lavinia's love.

DEMETRIUS taunts his younger brother and dares him to attack. When **CHIRON** takes a swing, **DEMETRIUS** grabs and twists his arm forcing **CHIRON** onto his hands and knees.

AARON (*aside to the camera*)
Clubs, clubs! these lovers will not keep the peace.

DEMETRIUS straddles **CHIRON**'s back, grabs his hair and yanks his face upwards.

DEMETRIUS
Why, boy, although our mother, unadvised,
Gave you a dancing-rapier by your side,
Are you so desperate grown to threat your friends?
Go to; have your lath glued within your sheath
Till you know better how to handle it.

Mustering all his strength, **CHIRON** manages to jump up, throwing **DEMETRIUS** off of his back.

CHIRON
Meanwhile, sir, with what little skill I have,
Full well shalt thou perceive how much I dare.

CHIRON gives a quick jab to **DEMETRIUS**' face, delivering him a bloody nose.

DEMETRIUS (*finally pissed*)
Ay, boy, grow ye so brave?

They both draw knives out of the tops of their boots and just as they go for each other, **AARON** comes forward, catches their wrists in mid-air and twists their arms, causing the knives to drop and both **BOYS** to kneel on the floor.

AARON (*still holding on to them*)
Why, how now, lords!
Here in the emperor's palace dare you draw,
And maintain such a quarrel openly?
Full well I wot the ground of all this grudge:
I would not for a million of gold
The cause were known to them it most concerns;
Nor would your noble mother for much more
Be so dishonour'd in the court of Rome.
For shame, put up.

He lets go of them. **DEMETRIUS** jumps up and retrieves his knife though **AARON**'s presence stops him from any action.

DEMETRIUS
Not I, till I have sheathed
My rapier in his bosom, and withal
Thrust these reproachful speeches down his throat
That he hath breathed in my dishonour here.

CHIRON
For that I am prepared and full resolved,
Foul-spoken coward, that thunder'st with thy tongue,
And with thy weapon nothing darest perform.

They go for each other but **AARON**, like a flash, steps between them.

AARON (*thunders*)
Away, I say!

Nervous that they will wake up the rest of the palace, **AARON** grabs the two **BOYS** by their necks and . . .

INT. CORRIDOR OF THE PALACE — EARLY MORNING

. . . forces them to walk through the corridor en route to a private room.

From time to time a **SERVANT** will cross their path and disappear into a room.

AARON (*continuing in an intense, hushed voice*)
Now, by the gods that warlike Goths adore,
This petty brabble will undo us all.

INT. PALACE HALL — EARLY MORNING

    AARON continues to guide them up the stairs and down the hallways.

AARON (*cont'd*)
Why, lords, and think you not how dangerous
It is to step upon a prince's right?
What, is Lavinia, then, become so loose,
Or Bassianus so degenerate,
That for her love such quarrels may be broach'd
Without controlment, justice, or revenge?
Young lords, beware! an should the empress know
This discord's ground, the music would not please.

    CHIRON breaks away and bounces down the hall in front of AARON
    and DEMETRIUS like a young puppy.

CHIRON
I care not, I, knew she and all the world.

    He leans precariously over a balustrade at the top of the inner stair-
    well.

CHIRON (*cont'd*)
I love Lavinia more than all the world.

    DEMETRIUS catches his foot, lifts it high, causing CHIRON to almost
    fall over the railing headfirst.

DEMETRIUS
Youngling, learn thou to make some meaner choice;
Lavinia is thine elder brother's hope.

> AARON grabs CHIRON's other leg and pulls him back onto safe
> ground. He turns to DEMETRIUS.

AARON
Why, are ye mad? or know ye not, in Rome
How furious and impatient they be,
And cannot brook competitors in love?

> AARON opens the door to a bedroom and shoves the TWO BOYS inside.

INT. BEDROOM — EARLY MORNING

> He closes and bolts the door.

AARON (*continuing*)
I tell you, lords, you do but plot your deaths
By this device.

> CHIRON leaps onto the bed, playing dead, then
> grabs a huge pillow and embraces it.

CHIRON
Aaron, a thousand deaths
Would I propose to achieve her whom I love.

AARON (*sarcastically*)
To achieve her!—how?

DEMETRIUS
Why makest thou it so strange?
She is a woman, therefore may be woo'd;
She is a woman, therefore may be won;
She is Lavinia, therefore must be loved.

> He makes an obscene gesture with his crotch
> that is enjoyed by CHIRON.

AARON (*turning back*)
Why, then, it seems, some certain snatch or so
Would serve your turns.

> CHIRON rolls to the edge of the bed.

CHIRON
Ay, so the turn were served.

DEMETRIUS
Aaron, thou hast hit it.

Why makest thou it so strange?
She is a woman,
therefore may be woo'd;
She is a woman,
therefore may
be won;
She is . . .
Lavinia,
therefore must
be loved.

AARON
Would you had hit it too!
Then should not we be tired with this ado.
Are you such fools
To square for this? would it offend you, then,
That both should speed?

CHIRON
Faith, not me.

DEMETRIUS
Nor me, so I were one.

AARON
For shame, be friends, and join for that you jar:
'Tis policy and stratagem must do
That you affect; and I have found the path.

> DEMETRIUS and CHIRON watch him as he walks to
> the window and looks out.

AARON (*cont'd*)
My lords, a solemn hunting is in hand;
There will be the lovely Roman ladies troop:
The forest-walks are wide and spacious;

> The two BOYS go to either side of AARON to look
> out the window.

AARON (*cont'd*)
And many unfrequented plots there are
Fitted by kind for rape and villainy:

> AARON turns around to look them straight in the eyes.

AARON (*cont'd*)
Single you thither, then, this dainty doe,
And strike her home by force, if not by words:
This way, or not at all, stand you in hope.

The two boys are shocked by AARON's plan. CHIRON is confused and looks to DEMETRIUS who becomes increasingly excited by the plan.

AARON (*cont'd*)
Come, come, our empress, with her sacred wit
Will we acquaint with all that we intend . . .

AARON moves to the door and unbolts it.

CHIRON and DEMETRIUS bolt to the door.

EXT. HUNTING GROUNDS — DAY

SATURNINUS, TAMORA, LAVINIA and BASSIANUS on horseback and chariot race down a steep slope surrounded by galloping soldiers and hunters. Wildly yelping dogs lead the hunt.

EXT. THE FOREST — DAY

AARON is crouched beside the trunk of a tree. Light filters through the leaves. He is digging a hole. In it he places a bag of gold.

AARON (*to camera*)
He that had wit would think that I had none,
To bury so much gold under a tree,
And never after to inherit it.
Let him that thinks of me so abjectly
Know that this gold must coin a stratagem,
Which, cunningly effected, will beget
A very excellent piece of villainy:
   (*back to burying the bag*)
And so repose, sweet gold, for their unrest

He pats the dirt.

AARON (*cont'd*)
That have their alms out of the empress' chest.

An arrow hits the tree right beside AARON's head. He draws his knife and turns to see TAMORA sitting on her WHITE HORSE, fifty feet away. She has a bow in her hand and is laughing. She dismounts from her horse, tethers it and playfully approaches AARON through the trees.

TAMORA
My lovely Aaron, wherefore look'st thou sad,
When every thing doth make a gleeful boast?
The birds chant melody on every bush;
The snake lies rolled in the cheerful sun;
The green leaves quiver with the cooling wind,
Under their sweet shade, Aaron, let us sit.

She takes off his coat, spreads it on the ground under the tree and flops down upon her back, reaching her hand up to take AARON's.

He allows her to pull him to his knees between her legs which she promptly and playfully curls around his body.

TAMORA (*cont'd*)
And—after conflict
We may, each wreathed in the other's arms,
Our pastimes done, possess a golden slumber;
Whiles hounds and horns and sweet melodious birds
Be unto us as is a nurse's song
Of lullaby to bring her babe asleep.

AARON is not seduced by her. As he speaks he remains kneeling upright, while she, frustrated, rolls onto her side with a sigh.

AARON
Madam, though Venus govern your desires,
Saturn is dominator over mine:
What signifies my deadly-standing eye,
My silence and my cloudy melancholy,
No, madam, these are no venereal signs!

TAMORA looks up at him, questioning. At his next word she sits up. As he continues to speak he takes her face into his hands and fondly kisses her forehead, her lips, her neck, her breasts, her hand.

AARON (*cont'd*)
Vengeance is in my heart, death in my hand,
Blood and revenge are hammering in my head.
Hark, Tamora, the empress of my soul,
Which never hopes more heaven than rests in thee,

He stops kissing her and looks directly into her eyes.

AARON (*cont'd*)
This is the day of doom for Bassianus:
His Philomel must lose her tongue to-day;
Thy sons make pillage of her chastity,
And wash their hands in Bassianus' blood.

He pulls a letter from his jacket.

AARON (*cont'd*)
Seest thou this letter? take it up, I pray thee,
And give the king this fatal-plotted scroll.
Now question me no more, we are espied.

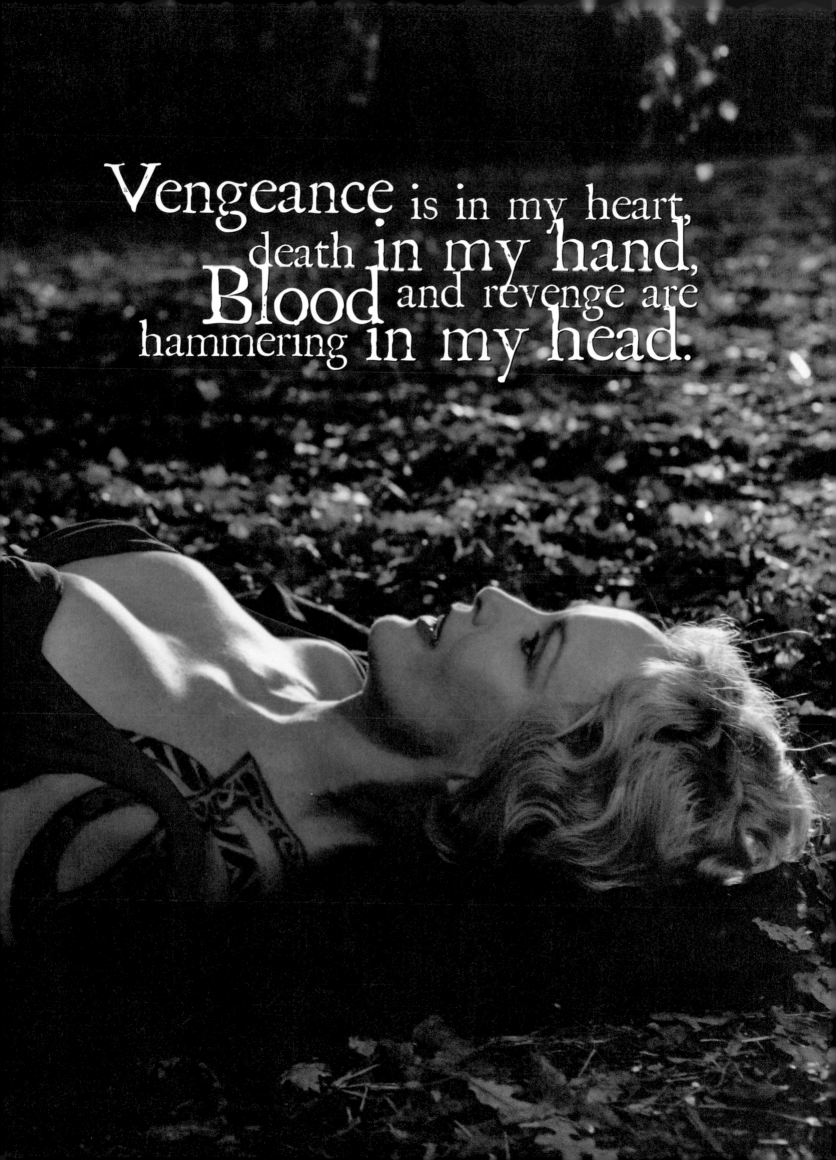

Vengeance is in my heart, death in my hand, Blood and revenge are hammering in my head.

BASSIANUS and LAVINIA, mounted on their horses, can be seen through the trees staring at them.

AARON jumps up and helps pull TAMORA to her feet.

TAMORA (*kissing him as he breaks away*)
Ah, my sweet Moor, sweeter to me than life!

AARON
No more, great empress, Bassianus comes:
Be cross with him; and I'll go fetch thy sons
To back thy quarrels, whatsoe'er they be.

He backs away from her bowing his head subserviently and then disappears into the woods.

BASSIANUS and LAVINIA have dismounted from their horses and approach TAMORA.

BASSIANUS
Who have we here? Rome's royal empress,
Unfurnish'd of her well-beseeming troop?

Or is it Dian, habited like her,
Who hath abandoned her holy groves
To see the general hunting in this forest?

TAMORA (*turning on him*)
Saucy controller of our private steps!
Had I the power that some say Dian had,
Thy temples should be planted presently
With horns, as was Acteon's; and the hounds
Should drive upon thy new-transformed limbs,
Unmannerly intruder as thou art!

LAVINIA
Under your patience, gentle empress,
'Tis thought you have a goodly gift in horning;
And to be doubted that your Moor and you
Are singled forth to try experiments:
Jove shield your husband from his hounds to-day!
'Tis pity they should take him for a stag.

BASSIANUS
Why are you sequester'd from all your train,
Dismounted from your snow-white goodly steed,
And wander'd hither to an obscure plot,
Accompanied but with a barbarous Moor,
If foul desire had not conducted you?

LAVINIA
And, being intercepted in your sport,
Great reason that my noble lord be rated
For sauciness.—I pray you, let us hence,

And let her joy her raven-colour'd love;
This valley fits the purpose passing well.

They start to go to their horses but **BASSIANUS** *turns back for a last dig.*

BASSIANUS
The King my brother shall have notice of this.

LAVINIA
Good king, to be so mightily abused!

TAMORA (*to herself*)
Why have I patience to endure all this?

She screams.

The horses of **LAVINIA** *and* **BASSIANUS** *run away, untethered by* **DEMETRIUS** *who surprises the couple with his sudden appearance, blocking their path. As they turn to go another way they are confronted by a grinning* **CHIRON**.

DEMETRIUS, *by now, has run to his mother who collapses into his arms.*

DEMETRIUS
How now, dear sovereign and our gracious mother!
Why doth your highness look so pale and wan?

TAMORA
Have I not reason, think you, to look pale?
These two have 'ticed me hither to this place.

BASSIANUS and LAVINIA turn to TAMORA, incredulous at what she is saying. As she continues to tell her tale she rises and begins to circle the confused and slightly bemused couple.

TAMORA (*cont'd*)
A barren detested vale you see it is;
And when they show'd me this abhorred pit,
They told me, here, at dead time of the night,
A thousand fiends, a thousand hissing snakes,
Ten thousand swelling toads,
Would make such fearful and confused cries,
As any mortal body hearing it
Should straight fall mad, or else die suddenly.

Subtly, the tenor of TAMORA's ranting becomes uncomfortably threatening for BASSIANUS and LAVINIA. They try to leave but are stopped by DEMETRIUS who puts his arms around their shoulders, forcing them to turn back and face his mother as she raves on.

TAMORA (*cont'd*)
No sooner had they told this hellish tale,
But straight they told me they would bind me here
And leave me to this miserable death:
And then they call'd me foul adulteress,
Lascivious Goth, and all the bitterest terms
That ever ear did hear to such effect:
And, had you not by wondrous fortune come,
This vengeance on me had they executed.
Revenge it, as you love your mother's life,
Or be ye not henceforth call'd my children.

DEMETRIUS
This is a witness that I am thy son.

    He stabs BASSIANUS in the back.

CHIRON
And this for me, struck home to show my strength.

    He stabs BASSIANUS in the belly. LAVINIA falls to her knees over her
    dead husband. She then challenges TAMORA.

LAVINIA
Ay, come, Semiramis,—nay, barbarous Tamora,
For no name fits thy nature but thy own!

    TAMORA grabs the knife from DEMETRIUS' hand and goes for
    LAVINIA.

TAMORA
Give me the poniard;
Your mother's hand shall right your mother's wrong.

DEMETRIUS (*stopping his mother*)
Stay, madam; here is more belongs to her;
First thrash the corn, then after burn the straw:
This minion stood upon her chastity,
Upon her nuptial vow, her loyalty,
And with that painted hope she braves your mightiness:
And shall she carry this unto her grave?

CHIRON (*stroking Lavinia's hair*)
An if she do, I would I were an eunuch.
Drag hence her husband to some secret hole,
And make his dead trunk pillow to our lust.

> DEMETRIUS drags the body of BASSIANUS away from LAVINIA.

TAMORA
But when ye have the honey ye desire,
Let not this wasp outlive us all to sting.

CHIRON
I warrant you, madam, we will make that sure.
Come, mistress, now perforce we will enjoy
That nice-preserved honesty of yours.

LAVINIA
O Tamora! thou bear'st a woman's face.

TAMORA
I will not hear her speak; away with her!

LAVINIA
Sweet lords, entreat her hear me but a word.

DEMETRIUS
Listen, fair madam: let it be your glory
To see her tears; but be your heart to them
As unrelenting flint to drops of rain.

LAVINIA
When did the tiger's young ones teach the dam?
O, do not learn her wrath, she taught it thee;
The milk thou suck'dst from her did turn to marble;
Yet every mother breeds not sons alike:
    (*To Chiron*)
Do thou entreat her show a woman pity.

CHIRON
What, wouldst thou have me prove myself a bastard?

> During the following desperate plea LAVINIA, on her knees, tries to crawl away. DEMETRIUS, amused by the pathetic sight, catches the hem of her skirt to keep her from escaping. Tauntingly he pulls off each of her shoes, tossing them to CHIRON. He then takes his knife and pops off each of the buttons on the back of her blouse. CHIRON, in a nervous state of agitation, violently rips LAVINIA's blouse from her shoulders.

LAVINIA
O, be to me, though thy hard heart say no,
Nothing so kind, but something pitiful!

TAMORA
I know not what it means. Away with her!

> The BOYS pick her up and start to carry her off.

LAVINIA
O, let me teach thee! for my father's sake,
That gave thee life, when well he might have slain thee.

TAMORA
Hadst thou in person ne'er offended me,
Even for his sake am I pitiless.—
Remember, boys, I pour'd forth tears in vain
To save your brother from the sacrifice;
But fierce Andronicus would not relent:
Therefore, away with her, use her as you will;
The worse to her, the better loved of me.

> LAVINIA breaks away from the two BOYS and rushes to TAMORA, grabbing her skirts.

LAVINIA
O Tamora, be call'd a gentle queen,
And with thine own hands kill me in this place!
And tumble me into some loathsome pit,
Where never man's eye may behold my body.
Do this, and be a charitable murderer.

TAMORA
So should I rob my sweet sons of their fee:
No, let them satisfy their lust on thee.

DEMETRIUS
Away! for thou hast stay'd us here too long.

> **CHIRON** grabs her again, dragging her away. She turns back for one last word to **TAMORA**.

LAVINIA
No grace? no womanhood? Ah, beastly creature!
Confusion fall!

CHIRON (*smacking her across the face*)
Nay, I'll stop your mouth.

TAMORA
Farewell, my sons: see that you make her sure.

> **DEMETRIUS** and **CHIRON** disappear into the woods with **LAVINIA**.

TAMORA (*cont'd*) (*to herself*)
Ne'er let my heart know merry cheer indeed
Till all the Andronici be made away.
Now will I hence to seek my lovely Moor,
And let my spleenful sons this trull deflow'r.

EXT. ANOTHER PART OF THE FOREST — LATE AFTERNOON

> **AARON** appears followed by **QUINTUS** and **MARTIUS**. The boys move cautiously through the dappled woods, their crossbows ready for action.

> A **DOE** is spotted in a distant clearing. She freezes. The boys raise their weapons. She darts away.

AARON
Come on, my lords, the better foot before:
Straight will I bring you to the loathsome pit
Where I espied the tiger fast asleep.

> They have a hard time keeping up with **AARON**. He leads them to
> the pit from the previous scene. It is camouflaged.

QUINTUS
My sight is very dull, whate'er it bodes.

MARTIUS
And mine, I promise you; were it not for shame,
Well could I leave our sport to sleep awhile.

> A **TIGER**, barely visible, disappears behind a tree.

> **MARTIUS** catches a glimpse of **AARON** and falls into the pit.

MARTIUS (*cont'd*)
(*Shouts as he falls—and moans*)

QUINTUS
What, art thou fall'n?—What subtle hole is this,
Whose mouth is cover'd with rude-growing briers,
Upon whose leaves are drops of new-shed blood
Speak, brother, hast thou hurt thee with the fall?

MARTIUS
O brother, with the dismall'st object hurt
That ever eye with sight made heart lament!

> **AARON** smirks to the camera and steals away.

MARTIUS (*cont'd*)
Why dost not comfort me, and help me out
From this unhallow'd and blood-stained hole?

QUINTUS
My heart suspects more than mine eye can see.

MARTIUS
To prove thou hast a true-divining heart,
Aaron and thou look down into this den,
And see a fearful sight of blood and death.

QUINTUS (*looking about for Aaron*)
Aaron is gone.

> From inside the pit a thin shaft of light shows us that **MARTIUS** has
> fallen on **BASSIANUS'** body.

MARTIUS
Lord Bassianus lies embrewed here,
All on a heap, like to a slaughter'd lamb.
O brother, help me!

> QUINTUS leans over the pit and reaches his hand down as far as he can. MARTIUS strains to clasp his hand.

QUINTUS
I have no strength to pluck thee to the brink.

> QUINTUS falls into the dark pit.

EXT. THE FOREST — LATE AFTERNOON

> SATURNINUS follows AARON on the path to the pit. HUNTSMEN also attend.

SATURNINUS (*jokingly*)
Along with me: I'll see what hole is here,
And what he is that now is leap'd into it.

> AARON brings him to the edge of the pit.

SATURNINUS (*cont'd*)
Say, who art thou that lately didst descend
Into this gaping hollow of the earth?

QUINTUS (*from within*)
The unhappy son of old Andronicus;
Brought hither in a most unlucky hour,
To find thy brother Bassianus dead.

SATURNINUS
Hmmm . . . oh!
My brother dead! I know thou dost but jest:
He and his lady both are at the lodge
'Tis not an hour since I left him there.

> He leans down to notice the blood on the leaves around the pit, and now on the palm of his hand.

TAMORA (O.S.)
Where is my lord the king?

> Enter TAMORA; then TITUS, LUCIUS and MARCUS.

SATURNINUS
Here, Tamora; though grieved with killing grief.

TAMORA
Where is thy brother Bassianus?

SATURNINUS
Now to the bottom dost thou search my wound:
Poor Bassianus here lies murdered.

TAMORA
Then all too late I bring this fatal writ.
  (*she reads*)
"An if we miss to meet him handsomely,
Sweet huntsman, Bassianus 'tis we mean,
Do thou so much as dig the grave for him:
Thou know'st our meaning. Look for thy reward . . ."

  SATURNINUS takes the letter from TAMORA.

SATURNINUS
"Among the nettles at the elder-tree
Which overshades the mouth of that same pit
Where we decreed to bury Bassianus.
Do this, and purchase us thy lasting friends."
O Tamora! was ever heard the like?

TAMORA
This is the pit, and this the elder-tree.

SATURNINUS
Look, sirs, if you can find the huntsman out
That should have murder'd Bassianus here.

  AARON has dug out the bag of gold that he had planted at the base
  of the tree.

AARON
My gracious lord, here is the bag of gold.

  TAMORA goes to AARON to get the gold. They secretly exchange
  smiles.

SATURNINUS (*to Titus*)
Two of thy whelps, fell curs of bloody kind,
Have here bereft my brother of his life.
  (*to Huntsmen*)
Sirs, drag them from the pit unto the prison:
There let them bide until we have devised
Some never-heard-of torturing pain for them.

  The HUNTSMEN take ropes and begin to set up the rigging by
  throwing them over the branch of a tree.

TITUS
High emperor, upon my feeble knee

I beg this boon, with tears not lightly shed,
That this fell fault of my accursed sons,
Accursed, if the fault be proved in them . . .

SATURNINUS
If it be proved! you see it is apparent.
Who found this letter? Tamora, was it you?

TAMORA
Andronicus himself did take it up.

TITUS
I did, my lord: yet let me be their bail;
For, by my father's reverend tomb, I vow
They shall be ready at your highness' will
To answer their suspicion with their lives.

SATURNINUS
Thou shalt not bail them: see thou follow me.
Some bring the murder'd body, some the murderers:
Let them not speak a word, the guilt is plain;
For, by my soul, were there worse end than death,
That end upon them should be executed.

    SATURNINUS leaves with the **HUNTSMEN**.

    TITUS and **LUCIUS** watch as **THE BOYS** and **BASSIANUS** are hoisted
    out of the pit in a net.

TAMORA
Andronicus, I will entreat the king:
Fear not thy sons; they shall do well enough.

She leaves, followed by AARON.

TITUS
Come, Lucius, come; stay not to talk with them.

EXT. A SWAMP ON THE EDGE OF THE FOREST — DUSK

A forest fire has ravaged a clearing. Charred tree stumps stand stark against the fading light of day. In the distance two figures dance wildly about a third who is perched on top of a four-foot tree stump.

On coming closer we see it is LAVINIA on top of the tree stump. In place of her cut-off hands are sprays of broken twigs. Her torn and tattered petticoats are stained with blood.

DEMETRIUS and CHIRON, in a frenetic state of fear, agitation and exhilaration, are zipping up their pants, as they continue to taunt and physically threaten her.

DEMETRIUS
So, now go tell, an if thy tongue can speak,
Who 'twas that cut thy tongue and ravish'd thee.

CHIRON
Write down thy mind, bewray thy meaning so,
An if thy stumps will let thee play the scribe.

DEMETRIUS
See, how with signs and tokens she can scrowl.

CHIRON
Go home, call for sweet water—sweet water . . .

DEMETRIUS (*Yells in background.*)
Sweet water!

CHIRON
 . . . Wash thy hands.

DEMETRIUS
She hath no tongue to call, nor hands to wash;
And so let's leave her to her silent walks.

CHIRON
An 'twere my case, I should go hang myself.

DEMETRIUS
If thou hadst hands to help thee knit the cord.

They run off, leaving LAVINIA alone on the tree stump, unable to get down.

She hath
nor ha
And
leave
her

no tongue to call,
nds to wash;
so let's
her to
silent
walks.

The wind howls.

Through the trees MARCUS can see the distant figure standing on the stump in the middle of the clearing. He approaches.

MARCUS
Who is this? my niece!

LAVINIA, traumatized, looks at her uncle and then turns away in shame.

MARCUS (*cont'd*) (*to himself*)
If I do dream, would all my wealth would wake me!
If I do wake, some planet strike me down,
That I may slumber in eternal sleep!
    (*to her*)
Speak, gentle niece, what stern ungentle hands
Have lopp'd and hew'd and made thy body bare
Of her two branches, those sweet ornaments,
Whose circling shadows kings have sought to sleep in,
Why dost not speak to me?

LAVINIA turns suddenly to MARCUS to speak. Blood flows from her mouth, but no words. Her tongue has been cut out.

MARCUS reaches up to gently take LAVINIA off the tree and into his arms.

MARCUS (*cont'd*)
Come, let us go, and make thy father blind;
For such a sight will blind a father's eye:
One hour's storm will drown the fragrant meads;
What will whole months of tears thy father's eyes?
    (*she tries to get out of his arms*)
Do not draw back, for we will mourn with thee:
O, could our mourning ease thy misery!

He carries her out of the ravaged clearing.

EXT. A ROMAN ROAD — MORNING

An ancient cobblestone road on the edge of the city is lined by large broken columns. Apartment buildings and ruins grow side by side in the distance. A procession makes its way to the place of execution. We see only the backs of judges, tribunes, townspeople, etc. TITUS moves (towards the tracking camera) through the procession, pleading for the lives of his two condemned sons.

TITUS
Hear me, grave fathers! noble tribunes, stay!
For pity of mine age, whose youth was spent
In dangerous wars, whilst you securely slept;
For all my blood in Rome's great quarrel shed;
For all the frosty nights that I have watch'd;
And for these bitter tears, which now you see
Filling the aged wrinkles in my cheeks;
Be pitiful to my condemned sons,
Whose souls are not corrupted as 'tis thought.

> A primitive iron wagon carrying the two manacled prisoners, **MAR-TIUS** and **QUINTUS**, passes by **TITUS**. The boys look to their father for help but know it is useless. **TITUS** continues to plead with the **TRIBUNES**.

TITUS (*cont'd*)
For two-and-twenty sons I never wept,
Because they died in honour's lofty bed.
For these, these, tribunes, in the dust I write,

> He lies facedown in the dirt. Wagon wheels, chariot wheels, automobile wheels pass him by. Dust swirling.

TITUS (*cont'd*)
My heart's deep languor and my soul's sad tears:
Let my tears stanch the earth's dry appetite;
My sons' sweet blood will makc it shame and blush.

> The procession has left **TITUS** alone, prostrate on the road, weeping. He is at a crossroads.

> The sound of a funereal trumpet is heard in the distance.

> Coming along the road marches the figure of an angel, a **YOUNG GIRL**, in black, playing the trumpet, heralding the vision of:

PENNY ARCADE NIGHTMARE #2

> **TITUS'** head rises to fill the frame. As we move into his eye, the Angel flies by to reveal an altar at the end of the road. On it is a sacrificial lamb.

> As a knife approaches the body of the lamb, its head transforms into the face of **MUTIUS**.

> Suddenly a myriad of angels fill the screen, their trumpets blaring, voices crying. As we move into the black hole of a single trumpet, the camera spirals downwards to reveal **TITUS** lying prostrated in the center of the crossroads.

EXT. A ROMAN ROAD — MORNING

TITUS
O earth, I shall befriend thee more with rain,
That shall distil from these two ancient urns,
Than youthful April shall with all his showers;
In summer's drought I'll drop upon thee still;
In winter with warm tears I'll melt the snow,
And keep eternal spring-time on thy face,
So thou refuse to drink my dear sons' blood.

> LUCIUS, who has just come running from the direction of the execution site, stops to see his father in the distance, facedown on the road. He watches as TITUS rises, walking on his knees, hands outstretched, pleading to invisible figures.

TITUS (*cont'd*)
O reverend tribunes! O gentle, aged men!
Unbind my sons, reverse the doom of death;
And let me say, that never wept before,
My tears are now prevailing orators.

> LUCIUS has come up behind his father.

LUCIUS
O noble father, you lament in vain:
The tribunes hear you not; no man is by;
And you recount your sorrows to a stone.

TITUS
Ah, Lucius, for thy brothers let me plead.
Grave tribunes, once more I entreat of you.

LUCIUS
My gracious lord, no tribune hears you speak.

TITUS
Why, 'tis no matter, man: if they did hear,
They would not mark me; or if they did mark,

Therefore I tell my SORROWS

to the stones

They would not pity me.
Therefore I tell my sorrows to the stones;
A stone is soft as wax, tribunes more hard than stones;
A stone is silent, and offendeth not,
And tribunes with their tongues doom men to death.

He rises to his feet with the help of LUCIUS.

TITUS (*cont'd*)
But wherefore stand'st thou with thy weapon drawn?

LUCIUS
To rescue my two brothers from their death:
For which attempt the judges have pronounced
My everlasting doom of banishment.

TITUS
O happy man! they have befriended thee.
Why, foolish Lucius, dost thou not perceive
That Rome is but a wilderness of tigers?
Tigers must prey; and Rome affords no prey
But me and mine: how happy art thou, then,
From these devourers to be banished!
But who comes with our brother Marcus here?

Coming towards them are MARCUS and LAVINIA, her uncle's coat wrapped around her.

MARCUS
Titus, prepare thy aged eyes to weep;
Or, if not so, thy noble heart to break:
I bring consuming sorrow to thine age.

TITUS
Will it consume me? let me see it, then.

He removes the coat from LAVINIA, exposing her cut-off hands.

MARCUS
This was thy daughter.

LUCIUS
(*Sighs and turns away.*)

TITUS
Why, Marcus, so she is.

LUCIUS (*falling to his knees*)
This object kills me!

TITUS (*harshly*)
Faint-hearted boy, arise, and look upon her.
Speak, Lavinia, what accursed hand
Hath made thee handless in thy father's sight?
What fool hath added water to the sea,
Or brought a torch to bright-burning Troy?
My grief was at the height before thou camest;
And now, like Nilus, it disdaineth bounds.

> He rushes to LUCIUS to grab his sword. They struggle but LUCIUS
> is able to keep him from the sword.

TITUS (*cont'd*)
Give me a sword, I'll chop off my hands too;
For they have fought for Rome, and all in vain;
In bootless prayer have they been held up,
And they have served me to effectless use.
Now all the service I require of them
Is, that the one will help to cut the other.

...let us, that have our tongues, Plot some device of further misery...

LUCIUS
Speak, gentle sister, who hath martyr'd thee?

>   LAVINIA opens her mouth, exposing the fact that she has no tongue.

MARCUS
O, that delightful engine of her thoughts,
Is torn from forth that pretty hollow cage.

>   She breaks away from her uncle and starts to wander down one of
>   the crossroads.

LUCIUS (*interrupting Marcus*)
O, say thou for her, who hath done this deed?

MARCUS
O, thus I found her, straying in the park,
Seeking to hide herself, as doth the deer
That hath received some unrecuring wound.

>   TITUS, MARCUS, LUCIUS and LAVINIA are by now all separated, each
>   on one of the four connecting roads. The following monologue will
>   begin very close and inwards on TITUS.

TITUS
It was my deer; and he that wounded her
Hath hurt me more than had he kill'd me dead:
For now I stand as one upon a rock,
Environ'd with a wilderness of sea.
This way to death my wretched sons are gone;
Here stands my other son, a banish'd man;
And here my brother, weeping at my woes.
But that which gives my soul the greatest spurn,
Is dear Lavinia, dearer than my soul.

>   LAVINIA turns to look at her father.

TITUS (*cont'd*)
Gentle daughter, let me kiss thy lips;

>   Horrified at the idea she turns away from TITUS.

TITUS (*cont'd*)
Or make some sign how I may do thee ease.

>   Desperately TITUS looks about him for an answer. LAVINIA has
>   kneeled down in the road, gazing at herself in a large puddle. He
>   motions for the others to join him and LAVINIA around the muddy
>   water.

TITUS (*cont'd*)
Shall thy good uncle, and thy brother Lucius,
And thou, and I, sit round about some fountain,
Looking all downwards, to behold our cheeks
How they are stain'd, like meadows, by a flood,
Or shall we cut away our hands, like thine?
Or shall we bite our tongues, and in dumb-shows
Pass the remainder of our hateful days?
What shall we do? let us, that have our tongues,
Plot some device of further misery,
To make us wonder'd at in time to come.

The image of the family of four huddled together is reflected in the puddle.

Ripples in the water wipe out the reflection as it begins to rain.

DISSOLVE TO:

It is still raining. **YOUNG LUCIUS** peers out of the second-story window. He sees:

A dark figure under an umbrella walking up to the front door. It is **AARON**.

From the distance we see him bang on the door. The door opens. A **SERVANT** listens to what **AARON** has to say, shakes her head "No" and then closes the door.

He turns to go but turns back momentarily to see **YOUNG LUCIUS** watching him from the window.

TITUS, **LAVINIA**, **MARCUS** and **LUCIUS** come through the gate, drenched to the bone. They are confronted by **AARON**. In a hurry to get out of the rain they almost ignore what he is saying as he follows them up the path to the door.

AARON
Titus Andronicus, my lord the emperor
Sends thee this word, that, if thou love thy sons,
Let Marcus, Lucius, or thyself, old Titus,
Or any one of you, chop off your hand,
And send it to the king;

Everyone stops dead in their tracks. They are inside the house by now while **AARON** stands in the doorway.

AARON (*cont'd*)
He for the same
Will send thee hither both thy sons alive;
And that shall be the ransom for their fault.

> **LUCIUS** and **MARCUS** are aghast at **AARON**'s words, but **TITUS** enthusiastically ushers him into the house and closes the front door.

INT. TITUS' HOUSE — LATE DAY

> In the entrance.

TITUS
O gracious emperor! O gentle Aaron!
Did ever raven sing so like a lark,
With all my heart, I'll send his majesty my hand.
Good Aaron, wilt thou help to chop it off?

> He grabs **AARON** by the arm and leads him down a hallway leading to the inner courtyard. **LUCIUS** and **MARCUS** chase after them.

EXT. INNER COURTYARD — LATE DAY

> **YOUNG LUCIUS** is behind a pillar, listening.

LUCIUS (*chasing after Titus*)
Stay, father! for that noble hand of thine,
That hath thrown down so many enemies,
Shall not be sent: my hand will serve the turn,
My youth can better spare my blood than you:
And therefore mine shall save my brothers' lives.

MARCUS (*following Lucius and overlapping dialogue*)
Which of your hands hath not defended Rome,
And rear'd aloft the bloody battle-axe,
My hand hath been but idle; let it serve
To ransom my two nephews from their death.

They are in the inner courtyard. TITUS suddenly stops for a moment,
looks at the rain falling.

AARON turns to MARCUS and LUCIUS.

AARON
Nay, come, agree whose hand shall go along,
For fear they die before their pardon come.

MARCUS
My hand shall go.

LUCIUS
By heaven, it shall not go!

MARCUS (*to Titus*)
Now let me show a brother's love to thee.

TITUS (*turning to them*)
Agree between you; I will spare my hand.

LUCIUS
Then I'll go fetch an axe.

MARCUS
But I will use the axe.

They run across the courtyard in the rain towards a stone shed.

INT. TITUS' PANTRY — DAY

TITUS quickly motions for AARON to follow him.

TITUS
Come hither, Aaron; I'll deceive them both.
Lend me thy hand, and I will give thee mine.

TITUS enters the kitchen, AARON follows.

AARON (*aside to camera*)
If that be call'd deceit, I will be honest.

INT. THE KITCHEN — LATE DAY

TITUS shoos the COOK out of the room. He rolls up his sleeve and
lays his arm out in front of him in the midst of the food that the
COOK was preparing on the counter.

The door to the kitchen opens slightly to reveal
YOUNG LUCIUS secretly watching the action.

AARON deliberates over the various choices he has in kitchen utensils; poultry scissors next to a plucked chicken, a paring knife buried in potato peels, a bread knife, etc. He finally comes upon a meat cleaver. Perfect.

YOUNG LUCIUS watches as **AARON** shoves a butcher block under **TITUS'** arm and proceeds to chop off his hand.

The camera stays on the boy's face as **TITUS** yells in pain.

LUCIUS and **MARCUS** burst through another door to the kitchen. **LUCIUS** carries the axe. He stops at the sight, not believing his eyes.

MARCUS rushes to **TITUS'** aid. He quickly grabs dish towels to stop the bleeding.

TITUS (*in incredible pain*)
Now stay your strife: what shall be is dispatch'd.
Good Aaron, give his majesty my hand:
Tell him it was a hand that warded him
from thousand danger; bid him bury it;
As for my sons, say I account of them
As jewels purchased at an easy price.

    AARON places **TITUS'** hand in a Ziploc bag.
    LUCIUS glares at him.

AARON
I go, Andronicus: and for thy hand
Look by and by to have thy sons with thee.

    He bows to everyone, then turns to exit
    through the door behind which hides **YOUNG**
    LUCIUS. He frightens the boy as he strides past
    him, speaking directly to the tracking camera.

INT. AND EXT. TITUS' HOUSE — LATE DAY

AARON (*continuing*)
Their heads, I mean. O, how this villainy
Doth fat me with the very thoughts of it!
Let fools do good, and fair men call for grace,
Aaron will have his soul black like his face.

    By the end of this speech **AARON** has exited the front door, entered
    his black roadster, placed the bag with the hand under the rearview
    mirror and hit the gas.

If there were reason for these miseries, Then into limits could I bind my woes.

The car whizzes away. Radio music blasting.

EXT. THE INNER COURTYARD — NIGHT

> It has stopped raining. TITUS kneels on the muddy ground. LAVINIA watches him from under the dripping eaves. The others watch him from the portico.

TITUS
O, here I lift this one hand up to heaven,
And bow this feeble ruin to the earth.
If any power pities wretched tears,
To that I call!
(to Lavinia who has come to kneel next to him)
What, wouldst thou kneel with me?
Do, then, dear heart; for heaven shall hear our prayers;
Or with our sighs we'll breathe the welkin dim,
And stain the sun with fog, as sometime clouds
When they do hug him in their melting bosoms.

MARCUS
O brother, speak with possibility,
And do not break into these deep extremes.

TITUS
Are not my sorrows deep, having no bottom?
Then be my passions bottomless with them.

MARCUS
But yet let reason govern thy lament.

TITUS *(rising furiously)*
If there were reason for these miseries,
Then into limits could I bind my woes.
When heaven doth weep, doth not the earth o'erflow?
If the winds rage, doth not the sea wax mad,
Threat'ning the welkin with his big-swol'n face?
And wilt thou have a reason for this coil?

> LAVINIA rises and rushes into the arms of her father, weeping.

TITUS *(cont'd)*
I am the sea; hark, how her sighs do blow!
She is the weeping welkin, I the earth.
Then must my sea be moved with her sighs;
Then must my earth with her continual tears
Become a deluge, overflow'd and drown'd.
For why my bowels cannot hide her woes,
But like a drunkard must I vomit them.

Then give me leave; for losers will have leave
To ease their stomachs with their bitter tongues.

> The sound of up-tempo and crude carnival music can be heard in the distance.

EXT. IN FRONT OF TITUS' HOUSE — NIGHT

> THE CLOWN on his motorcycle, with a sideshow wagon attached, pulls up in front of TITUS' house. The carnival music blasts away.

> Meanwhile, YOUNG LUCIUS has opened the front door to see what all the racket is. TITUS, MARCUS, LUCIUS and LAVINIA, still in a state of deep turmoil, slowly exit from the front door, incredulous at the arrival of these grotesque entertainers.

> The YOUNG GIRL hops out of the vehicle and fetches some folding camp stools from inside the wagon. THE CLOWN barks Latin incantations from his megaphone while strutting and dancing to the music before his audience.

THE CLOWN (*in Latin*)
'Scopus legis est, aut eum quem punit emendet,
aut poena cius ceterus meliores reddet,
aut sublatis mails ceteri securiores vivant!'
[Which translates as: "The aim of the law is to correct those
it punishes, or make others better through the example of
the sentence it inflicts, or else to remove evil so that the
others can live more peacefully."]

> The YOUNG GIRL sets four stools in front of a mini-stage and kindly beckons for MARCUS, TITUS, LAVINIA and LUCIUS to sit, which they do. YOUNG LUCIUS observes from the archway.

> Timed to the music, the YOUNG GIRL and the CLOWN suddenly raise the red metal shutter door of the sideshow wagon revealing the mini-stage. There is an assault of silence at the sight of two heads (MARTIUS and QUINTUS) each floating in a glass specimen jar. Between the jarred heads on a mound of black velvet sits the amputated hand of TITUS. The "still life" is arranged on a quaint Victorian pedestal table.

> In a dry, emotionless tone THE CLOWN speaks over his megaphone.

THE CLOWN (*cont'd*)
Worthy Andronicus, ill art thou repaid
For that good hand thou sent'st the emperor.
Here are the heads of thy two noble sons;
And here's thy hand, in scorn to thee sent back.

MARCUS
　　(*violently rising from the stool and turning away from the sight*)
And be my heart an ever-burning hell!
These miseries are more than may be borne.

LUCIUS (*rising*)
Ah, that this sight should make so deep a wound,
And yet detested life not shrink thereat!

　　LAVINIA rises and goes to kiss TITUS.

MARCUS
Alas, poor heart, that kiss is comfortless
As frozen water to a starved snake.

TITUS (*still seated, looking at the heads*)
When will this fearful slumber have an end?

MARCUS (*finally angry*)
Die, Andronicus;
Thou dost not slumber: see, thy two sons' heads,
Thy warlike hand, thy mangled daughter here;
Thy other banish'd son, with this dear sight
Struck pale and bloodless; and thy brother, I,
Even like a stony image, cold and numb.
Ah, now no more will I control thy griefs,
Rent off thy silver hair, thy other hand
Gnawing with thy teeth; and be this dismal sight
The closing up of our most wretched eyes,
Now is a time to storm; why art thou still?

TITUS
Ha, ha, ha!

MARCUS
Why dost thou laugh?

When will this fearful slumber have an end?

TITUS
Why, I have not another tear to shed:
Besides, this sorrow is the enemy,
And would usurp upon my watery eyes,
And make them blind with tributary tears.
Then which way shall I find Revenge's cave?

> He goes up to the mini-stage and peers into it.

TITUS (*cont'd*)
For these two heads do seem to speak to me,
And threat me I shall never come to bliss
Till all these mischiefs be return'd again
Even in their throats that have committed them.

> He turns to the others, resolved.

TITUS (*cont'd*)
Now, let me see what task I have to do.
You heavy people, circle me about,
That I may turn me to each one of you,
And swear unto my soul to right your wrongs.

> They form a small circle around TITUS, their heads bowed as he
> slowly revolves, deliberately placing his palm on either the head or
> heart of each one of them.

TITUS (*cont'd*)
The vow is made.

> He goes up to the mini-stage and takes a jar with one of the heads,
> passes it to MARCUS and takes the other jar for himself.

TITUS (*cont'd*)
Come, brother, take a head;
And in this hand the other will I bear
And thou Lavinia, thou shalt be employ'd;
Bear thou my hand, sweet wench, between thy teeth.

> LAVINIA takes the hand in her mouth and she and MARCUS move to
> the house while TITUS goes to LUCIUS.

TITUS (*cont'd*)
As for thee, boy, go get thee from my sight,
Thou art an exile, and thou must not stay.
Hie to the Goths, and raise an army there.
And, if you love me, as I think you do,
Let's kiss and part, for we have much to do.

> They embrace.

LUCIUS watches his FAMILY enter the house and close the door.

LUCIUS
Farewell, Andronicus, my noble father,
The woefull'st man that ever liv'd in Rome.

YOUNG LUCIUS, who has watched the preceding events, runs to his father. LUCIUS hugs his child.

LUCIUS (*cont'd*)
Now will I to the Goths, and raise a power,
To be revenged on Rome and Saturnine.

INT. A WOODCARVER'S SHOP — DAY

A **WOODCARVER** sands the chipped paint from two wooden hands. He is surrounded by Saints and all sizes of classic religious and mythic icons. Behind him, on a shelf, rests a handless Madonna.

YOUNG LUCIUS picks up a pair of tiny wooden hands from a worktable laden with the wooden body parts of broken dolls and icons.

INT. TITUS' HOUSE — DAY

YOUNG LUCIUS enters the front door and runs down the corridor, looking for LAVINIA.

INT. SMALL INNER COURTYARD IN TITUS' HOUSE — SUNSET

LAVINIA sits alone in a corner of the small room.

YOUNG LUCIUS enters and cautiously goes to her. He presents a box, and proceeds to open it for her. A pair of wooden hands rests inside.

INT. TITUS' DINING ROOM — NIGHT

TWO SERVANTS lay out a meal on a large table.

TITUS, MARCUS, LAVINIA and YOUNG LUCIUS enter the room.

TITUS
So, so; now sit: and look you eat no more
Than will preserve just so much strength in us
As will revenge these bitter woes of ours.

Everyone sits. No one exhibits an appetite as the SERVANTS serve the food.

LAVINIA tries to communicate with MARCUS using her new wooden hands. Frustrated that he cannot understand, she turns her chair away from the table.

TITUS (*cont'd*) (*to Lavinia*)
Thou map of woe, that thus dost talk in signs!
When thy poor heart beats with outrageous beating,
Thou canst not strike it thus to make it still.
　(*he beats his chest with his fist*)
Wound it with sighing, girl, kill it with groans;
　(*he moves to her with a knife*)
Or get some little knife between thy teeth,
And just against thy heart make thou a hole;
That all the tears that thy poor eyes let fall
May run into that sink, and, soaking in,
Drown the lamenting fool in sea-salt tears.

MARCUS
Fie, brother, fie! Teach her not thus to lay
Such violent hands upon her tender life.

TITUS (*snapping sardonically*)
How now! Has sorrow made thee dote already?
Oh, handle not the theme, to talk of hands,
Lest we remember still that we have none.

Trying to remain under control, he pulls his chair next to LAVINIA and offers to feed her with a spoon.

TITUS (*cont'd*)
Come, let's fall to; and, gentle girl, eat this.

She rejects the food. Immediately he barks at the SERVANTS.

TITUS (*cont'd*)
Here is no drink!

LAVINIA again tries to express something.

TITUS (*cont'd*)
—Hark, Marcus, what she says;
I can interpret all her martyr'd signs;
She says she drinks no other drink but tears,
Speechless complainer, I will learn thy thought;
Thou shalt not sigh, nor hold thy stumps to heaven,
Nor wink, nor nod, nor kneel, nor make a sign,
But I of these will wrest an alphabet,
And by still practice learn to know thy meaning.

YOUNG LUCIUS strikes the table with a knife.

TITUS (*cont'd*) (*annoyed*)
What dost thou strike at, Lucius, with thy knife?

YOUNG LUCIUS
At that that I have kill'd, my lord,—a fly.

TITUS
Out on thee, murderer! thou kill'st my heart;
A deed of death done on the innocent
Becomes not Titus' grandson: get thee gone;
I see thou art not for my company.

> **YOUNG LUCIUS**, threatened, stands up, looking to **MARCUS** for help,
> but **MARCUS** is just as dismayed at **TITUS'** behavior.

YOUNG LUCIUS
Alas, my lord, I have but kill'd a fly.

TITUS
But how, if that fly had a father and mother?
How would he hang his slender gilded wings,
And buzz lamenting doings in the air!
   (*he picks up the dead fly*)
Poor harmless fly,
That, with his pretty buzzing melody,
Came here to make us merry! and thou hast kill'd him.

YOUNG LUCIUS
Pardon me, sir; it was a black ill-favour'd fly,
Like to the empress' Moor; therefore I kill'd him.

TITUS
O, O, O!
Pardon me for reprehending thee,

For thou hast done a charitable deed.
Give me thy knife, I will insult on him;
Flattering myself, as if it were the Moor
Come hither purposely to poison me.

> He has gotten the knife from a much relieved **YOUNG LUCIUS** and begins stabbing the dead fly.

TITUS (*cont'd*)
There's for thyself, and that's for Tamora.

> As he wildly stabs and stabs at the poor fly, a release of bittersweet laughter overtakes everyone.

TITUS (*cont'd*)
Ah, sirrah!
As yet, I think, we are not brought so low
But that between us we can kill a fly
That comes in likeness of a coal-black Moor.

INT. A DUNGEON IN THE PALACE — DAY

> A defunct torture chamber has been converted into a hangout by **DEMETRIUS** and **CHIRON**. They've got it set up with video games, a refrigerator and bar stocked with booze, a pool table and other amenities. The ancient torture devices have been preserved for their historical "quaintness." Some even make good workout apparatus.

> **DEMETRIUS** is hard at play at the standing video games. Seen from his back, he could be mercilessly fucking the machine, he's so into it—or out of it. From time to time he breaks away from the banging and the shaking to get a smoke or a beer.

> **CHIRON** madly dances around the room. Rock music blasting through his headphones.

> The two of them are frenetic, agitated, paranoid.

> **AARON**, on the contrary, stands very still at the pool table, cue stick in hand, contemplating his next move.

EXT. OLIVE GROVE — DAY

> **YOUNG LUCIUS**, carrying his schoolbooks under his arm, is being chased by **LAVINIA** through the olive trees behind **TITUS'** house. From afar it appears as fun, but up close we see that the boy is in a panic and frightened of his aunt.

EXT. THE GARDEN OF TITUS' HOUSE — DAY

> In the distance he sees **TITUS** and **MARCUS**. He drops his books and runs to them.

YOUNG LUCIUS
Help, grandsire, help! my aunt Lavinia
Follows me everywhere, I know not why.
Good uncle Marcus, see how swift she comes!
Alas, sweet aunt, I know not what you mean.

> LAVINIA has run past the fallen books, and right up to YOUNG
> LUCIUS.

MARCUS
Stand by me, Lucius; do not fear thine aunt.

> LAVINIA gesticulates wildly, leading them back to the books. She
> falls to her knees and tries to pick one up, turning it over with her
> wooden hands.

TITUS
How now, Lavinia! Marcus, what means this?

TITUS (*cont'd*)
Soft! so swiftly she turns the leaves!
Help her:
What would she find?—Lavinia, shall I read?

> YOUNG LUCIUS holds the book for her and TITUS leans over her
> shoulder to read.

TITUS (*cont'd*)
This is the tragic tale of Philomel,
And treats of Tereus' treason and his rape.

    Acknowledging the word, LAVINIA drops her head into the book
    and then begins wildly turning the pages with her teeth.

MARCUS
See, brother, see; note how she quotes the leaves.

TITUS
Lavinia, wert thou thus surprised, sweet girl,
Ravish'd and wrong'd, as Philomela was,
Forced in the ruthless, vast, and gloomy woods?

    LAVINIA shows him an illustration of a forest.

TITUS (*cont'd*)
Ay, such a place there is, where we did hunt.

MARCUS
O, why should nature build so foul a den,
Unless the gods delight in tragedies?

TITUS
Give signs, sweet girl,
What Roman lord it was durst do this deed.

    LAVINIA cries out with a harsh, unearthly sound. TITUS holds her.
    MARCUS, moved and frustrated, steps away searching for some solution.

MARCUS
My lord, look here!—look here, Lavinia:
This sandy plot is plain; guide, if thou canst,
This after me, when I have writ my name
Without the help of any hand at all.

    He writes his name in the sand with TITUS' staff, guiding it with only
    his arms and mouth.

MARCUS (*cont'd*)
Write thou, good niece; and here display, at last,
What God will have discover'd for revenge.

Apprehensive, **LAVINIA** moves to take the staff into her mouth.

MARCUS (*cont'd*)
Curst be that heart that forced us to this shift!

Just as her mouth opens wide for her lips to encircle the wood, a bolt of electric shock seems to run through her body.

PENNY ARCADE NIGHTMARE #3

Jolted instantaneously back into the moment of the rape, she violently rejects the staff from her mouth, letting it fall on her shoulder, and guides it with her arms.

LAVINIA's ferocious writing in the sand is intercut with a bombardment of surreal images of her rape and dismemberment.

We see her stripped to her torn petticoats, balanced on the top of a truncated column in the midst of a tinted black-and-white painted forest set. At times she appears to be part doe. Wind blows up her petticoats which she tries to keep down with her hooves. (It should remind us of the iconographic image of Marilyn Monroe holding her dress down over the subway grating.) Dried leaves also fly up with the wind.

At her feet, **DEMETRIUS** and **CHIRON**, half human and half ferocious tiger, attack and ravish the doe/woman.

Music stops.

As she finishes writing the last letter, she releases the staff.

TITUS
"Chiron. Demetrius."

MARCUS
My lord, kneel down with me; kneel, Lavinia;
And kneel, sweet boy, and swear with me,
That we will prosecute, by good advice,
Mortal revenge upon these traitorous Goths,
And see their blood, or die with this reproach.

TITUS
'Tis sure enough, an you knew how.
But if you hunt these bear-whelps, then beware:
    (*rising to his feet as a plan formulates in his mind*)
You are a young huntsman, Marcus; let alone;
Come, go with me into mine armoury;
Lucius, I'll fit thee; and withal, my boy
Shall carry from me to the empress' sons
Presents that I intend to send them both.
Come; thou'lt do thy message, wilt thou not?

YOUNG LUCIUS
Ay, with my dagger in their bosoms, grandsire.

TITUS
No, not so; I'll teach thee another course.
Lavinia, come.—Marcus, look to my house.

    The three leave **MARCUS** alone. He picks up the fallen staff.

MARCUS
O heavens, can you hear a good man groan,
And not relent, or not compassion him?
Marcus, attend him in his ecstasy,
That hath more scars of sorrow in his heart
Than foemen's marks upon his batter'd shield;
But yet so just that he will not revenge;
    (*shaking the staff in the air*)
Revenge, ye heavens, for old Andronicus!

INT. A DUNGEON IN THE PALACE — NIGHT

    YOUNG LUCIUS appears in the doorway with a bundle in his arms.
He is attended by **PUBLIUS**, one of **TITUS**' kinsmen. **CHIRON** seizes
on the opportunity for playful torment. He locks the door behind
the boy, shutting out **PUBLIUS**.

CHIRON
Demetrius, here's the son of Lucius;
He hath some message to deliver us.

DEMETRIUS
Ay, some mad message from his mad grandfather.

The boy tries to ignore the physical teasing of **CHIRON** and proceeds to deliver his speech with formality. **CHIRON** wants to know what's in the bundle.

YOUNG LUCIUS
My lords, with all the humbleness I may,
I greet your honours from Andronicus.

DEMETRIUS
Gramercy, lovely Lucius: what's the news?

> **DEMETRIUS** plucks a note from the bundle and unscrolls it.

> **CHIRON** has grabbed the bundle from **YOUNG LUCIUS** and proceeds to untie and unravel it on the table. Out falls a pile of archaic weapons from the dark ages. **CHIRON** is thrilled.

YOUNG LUCIUS (*cont'd*)
My grandsire, well advised, hath sent by me
The goodliest weapons of his armoury
To gratify your honourable youth,
The hope of Rome; for so he bid me say;
And so I do,
And so I leave you both,
    (*aside to camera*)
like bloody villains.

> **CHIRON** chases **YOUNG LUCIUS** out of the dungeon and returns to play with the weapons, trying each one out.

DEMETRIUS (*reading the scroll*)
"'Integer vitae, scelerisque purus,
Non eget Mauri iaculis, nec arcu.'"
'Nec arcu'?

CHIRON
O, 'tis a verse in Horace; I know it well:
"He who is pure of life and free of sin
Needs no bow and arrow of the Moor."

AARON (*from the corner*)
Ay, just,—a verse in Horace—right, you have it.
　(*aside to camera*)
Now, what a thing it is to be an ass!
Here's no sound jest! the old man hath found their guilt;
And sends them weapons wrapp'd about with lines
That wound, beyond their feeling, to the quick.
But were our witty empress well a-foot,
She would applaud Andronicus' conceit:
But let her rest in her unrest awhile.

　He approaches the two who are still engrossed with the gifts.

DEMETRIUS
Come, let us go; and pray to all the gods
To aid our mother in her labour pains.

AARON (*aside*)
Pray to the devils; the gods have given us over.

　A trumpet fanfare blasts.

DEMETRIUS (*pained and annoyed*)
Why do the emperor's trumpets flourish thus?

CHIRON (*sarcastic*)
Belike for joy the emperor hath a son.

DEMETRIUS
Soft! who comes here?

　CHIRON and **DEMETRIUS** hide at either side
　of the door. In the entrance stands the old
　NURSE with a small bundle wrapped in
　newspaper. At first it is not recognizable as
　an **INFANT**.

NURSE
Good morrow, lords:
O, tell me, did you see Aaron the Moor?

AARON (*calmly sitting with his feet up on the table*)
Well, more or less, or ne'er a whit at all,
Here Aaron is; and what with Aaron now?

NURSE (*goes to him*)
O gentle Aaron, we are all undone!
Now help, or woe betide thee evermore!

AARON
Why, what a caterwauling dost thou keep!
What dost thou wrap and fumble in thine arms?

NURSE
O, that which I would hide from heaven's eye,
Our empress' shame, and stately Rome's disgrace!
She is deliver'd, lords, she is deliver'd.

AARON
To whom?

> The boys get off on **AARON**'s punning, totally
> unnerving the **NURSE**.

NURSE
I mean, she is brought a-bed.

AARON
Well, God give her good rest. What hath he sent her?

NURSE
A devil.

AARON
Why, then she is the devil's dam;
A joyful issue.

NURSE
A joyless, dismal, black, and sorrowful issue.

> Everyone by now has crowded around the **NURSE** to see what is
> wrapped in the newspaper. **DEMETRIUS** and **CHIRON** are totally
> unprepared, while **AARON** is way ahead of the game. She rips off the
> paper to reveal the mulatto **INFANT**.

> **DEMETRIUS** and **CHIRON** back away in shock at the revelation.

NURSE (*cont'd*)
Here is the babe, as loathsome as a toad
Amongst the fairest breeders of our clime:
The empress sends it thee, thy stamp, thy seal,
And bids thee christen it with thy dagger's point.

AARON
’Zounds, ye whore! is black so base a hue?
Sweet blowse, you are a beauteous blossom, sure.

DEMETRIUS
Villain, what hast thou done?

AARON
That which thou canst not undo.

CHIRON
Thou hast undone our mother.

AARON
Villain, I have done thy mother.

DEMETRIUS
And therein, hellish dog, thou hast undone her.
Accurs’d the offspring of so foul a fiend!

CHIRON
It shall not live.

AARON
It shall not die.

NURSE
Aaron, it must; the mother wills it so.

AARON
What, must it, nurse? then let no man but I
Do execution on my flesh and blood.

DEMETRIUS
I’ll broach the tadpole on this rapier’s point.
Nurse, give it me; my sword shall soon dispatch it.

AARON
Sooner this sword shall plough thy bowels up.

    He grabs the scimitar from the table and with it smacks the sword
    out of DEMETRIUS’ hand.

AARON (*cont’d*)
Stay, murderous villains! will you kill your brother?
Now, by the burning tapers of the sky,
That shone so brightly when this boy was got,
He dies upon my scimitar’s sharp point
That touches this my first-born son and heir!
What, what, ye sanguine, shallow-hearted boys!
Ye white-limed walls! ye alehouse painted signs!

Coal-black is better than another hue,
In that it scorns to bear another hue;
For all the water of the ocean
Can never turn the swan's black legs to white,
Although she lave them hourly in the flood.

    He takes the **INFANT** *from the* **NURSE**.

AARON (*cont'd*)
Tell the empress from me, I am of age
To keep mine own, excuse it how she can.

DEMETRIUS
Wilt thou betray thy noble mistress thus?

AARON
My mistress is my mistress; this, myself,
The vigour and the picture of my youth:
This before all the world do I prefer
This spite of all the world will I keep safe,
Or some of you shall smoke for it in Rome.

DEMETRIUS
By this our mother is forever shamed.

NURSE
The emperor, in his rage, will doom her death.

CHIRON
I blush to think upon this ignomy.

AARON
Why, there's the privilege your beauty bears:
Fie, treacherous hue, that will betray with blushing
The close enacts and counsels of the heart!
Here's a young lad framed of another leer:

Coal-black is better than another hue, In that it scorns to bear another hue; For all the water of the ocean Can never turn the swan's black legs to white, Although she lave them hourly in the flood.

Look, how the black slave smiles upon the father,
As who should say, "Old lad, I am thine own."

NURSE
Aaron, what shall I say unto the empress?

DEMETRIUS
Advise thee, Aaron, what is to be done,
So we may all subscribe to thy advice.
Save thou the child, so we may all be safe.

AARON
Then sit we down, and let us all consult.
My son and I will have the wind of you:
Keep there! now talk at pleasure of your safety.

DEMETRIUS
How many women saw this child of his?

AARON
Ah, so, brave lords! when we join in league,
I am a lamb: but if you brave the Moor,
The chafed boar, the mountain lioness,
The ocean swells not so as Aaron storms.
But say, again, how many saw the child?

NURSE
Cornelia the midwife and myself;
And no one else but the deliver'd empress.

AARON
The empress, the midwife, and yourself:
Two may keep counsel when the third's away.
Go to the empress, tell her this I said:

    He suddenly stabs her. She screams and dies.

AARON (*cont'd*)
Weke, weke! so cries a pig prepared to the spit.

DEMETRIUS
What mean'st thou, Aaron? wherefore didst thou this?

AARON
O Lord, sir, 'tis a deed of policy:
Shall she live to betray this guilt of ours,
A long-tongued babbling gossip? no, lords, no:
Hark ye, lords; you see I have given her physic,
    (*pointing to the Nurse*)
You must needs bestow her funeral;

The fields are near, and you are gallant grooms:
This done, make sure you take no longer days,
But send the midwife presently to me.
The midwife and the nurse well made away,
Then let the ladies tattle what they please.

CHIRON
Aaron, I see thou wilt not trust the air
With secrets.

DEMETRIUS
For this care of Tamora,
Herself and hers are highly bound to thee.

> **DEMETRIUS** and **CHIRON** lift up the dead **NURSE** and drag her out of
> the room.

AARON (*aside to camera*)
Now to the Goths, as swift as swallow flies;
There to dispose this treasure in mine arms,
And secretly to greet the empress' friends.
> (*to Infant*)
Come on, you thick-lipp'd slave, I'll bear you hence;
For it is you that puts us to our shifts.
I'll make you feed on berries and on roots,
And cabin in a cave; and bring you up
To be a warrior and command a camp.

The goddess of justice has left the earth.

EXT. NARROW ROMAN STREET — 2 A.M.

Dressed in military armour and a bathrobe, **TITUS** marches down the dark cobbled streets. He is on a mission. **YOUNG LUCIUS** follows, pulling a red "radio flyer" wagon filled with tools and weapons.

They stop at a door. The boy knocks. A **SERVANT**, annoyed at being awakened, opens the door. Upon seeing **TITUS** she darts into the house.

PUBLIUS appears in the doorway, pulling his coat and hat on.

TITUS nods and starts marching. **PUBLIUS** joins **YOUNG LUCIUS** and follows.

EXT. ANOTHER SIDE STREET — 2:10 A.M.

SEMPRONIUS, another kinsman of **TITUS**, emerges from his house, zipping up his pants, putting on his hat, etc. He runs to join **PUBLIUS** and **YOUNG LUCIUS** who are still marching behind **TITUS**.

EXT. A WIDER STREET — 2:15 A.M.

CAIUS and **VALENTINE**, more kinsmen of **TITUS**, have joined the ranks and follow him down the dark city streets en route to the palace.

INT. PALACE ATRIUM — 2:15 A.M.

A giant, mosaic, heated pool dominates this opulent room decorated with erotic frescoes in Pompeian style. Under the open-air dome stirs the last vestiges of a wild party. Drunken, sleeping guests litter

the couches while some couples still frolic in the pool and others for-
nicate on the swinging beds and in silken hammocks.

DEMETRIUS floats with his naked consort on a mermaid raft, while
CHIRON enjoys a flesh-and-blood nymph.

PEACOCKS strut around the sleepy room.

INT. PALACE BEDROOM — NIGHT

A naked SATURNINUS sleeps contentedly on TAMORA's breast. She
gently strokes his head, unable to sleep.

EXT. ARCHWAY OUTSIDE THE PALACE — PRE-DAWN

YOUNG LUCIUS appears through an archway. He checks to see if any
guards are about, than signals back to TITUS and the others to come
ahead. MARCUS has joined the ranks.

TITUS
Come, Marcus, come: kinsmen, this is the way.

They cautiously follow YOUNG LUCIUS and TITUS through the gate-
way and into a courtyard facing the high palace wall. The KINSMEN
are unsure what to make of TITUS and his machinations but, out of
respect, they comply as he snaps them into military formation.

TITUS takes a bow and arrow from the wagon and hands it to
YOUNG LUCIUS.

TITUS (*cont'd*)
Sir boy, now let me see your archery;
Look ye draw home enough, and 'tis there straight.
The goddess of justice has left the earth.
Be you remember'd, Marcus, she's gone, she's fled.
Sirs, take you to your tools. You, cousins, shall

He grabs two fishing nets from the wagon and throws them to
CAIUS and VALENTINE.

TITUS (*cont'd*)
Go sound the ocean, and cast your nets;
Happily you may catch her in the sea;
Yet there's as little justice as at land:
No; Publius and Sempronius, you must do it;

TITUS hands them various digging tools from the wagon.

TITUS (*cont'd*)
'Tis you must dig with mattock and with spade,
And pierce the inmost centre of the earth:
Then, when you come to Pluto's region,

I pray you, give him this petition;
 (*taking a letter from his inside pocket and handing it to them*)
Tell him, it is for justice and for aid,
And that it comes from old Andronicus,
Shaken with sorrows in ungrateful Rome.

> The four perplexed men hesitate to move, not knowing what to make of TITUS' bizarre orders.

TITUS (*cont'd*) (*rambling to himself*)
Ah, Rome! Well, well; I made thee miserable
That time I threw the people's suffrages
On him that thus doth tyrannize o'er me.
 (*returning his attention to the men*)
Go, get you gone; and pray be careful all,
And leave you not a man-of-war unsearch'd:
This wicked emperor may have shipp'd her hence;
And, kinsmen, then we may go pipe for justice.

> The four MEN look to MARCUS for advice but he just signals for them to do TITUS' bidding. They exit through the archway.
>
> TITUS writes notes on pieces of paper and has YOUNG LUCIUS help tie the petitions around the ends of the arrows.
>
> For a second MARCUS watches his brother. Upset, he quickly strides through the archway.

EXT. THE OTHER SIDE OF THE ARCHWAY — PRE-DAWN

> MARCUS joins with PUBLIUS, CAIUS, SEMPRONIUS and VALENTINE to confer secretly.

MARCUS
O Publius, is not this a heavy case,
to see thy noble uncle thus distract?

PUBLIUS
Therefore, my lord, it highly us concerns
By day and night t'attend him carefully,
And feed his humour kindly as we may,
Till time beget some careful remedy.

MARCUS
Kinsmen, his sorrows are past remedy.

EXT. OUTSIDE THE PALACE — DAWN

> Stars are still visible in the sky.
>
> A pile of arrows bound with letters lies on the ground.

The **MEN** return through the archway.

TITUS
Publius, how now! how now, my masters!
You are a good archer, Marcus.—Come, to this gear;

He hands **MARCUS** an arrow.

TITUS (cont'd)
'Ad Jovem,' that's for you;

> One by one he gives each man an arrow while **YOUNG LUCIUS** helps
> distribute the bows.

TITUS (*cont'd*)
—here, 'Ad Apollinem';
Here, boy, "To Pallas"; here, "To Mercury";
"To Saturn," Caius, not to Saturnine;
You were as good to shoot against the wind.
To it, boy.—Marcus, loose when I bid.
Of my word, I have written to effect;
There's not a god left unsolicited.

> All of the **MEN** take aim, pointing their arrows in various directions
> towards the sky.

MARCUS
My lord, I aim a mile beyond the moon;
Your letter is with Jupiter by this.

TITUS
Marcus, we are but shrubs, no cedars we,
No big-boned men framed of the Cyclops' size;
But metal, Marcus, steel to the very back,
Yet wrung with wrongs more than our backs can bear:
And, sith there's no justice in earth nor hell,
We will solicit heaven, and move the gods
To send down Justice for to wreak our wrongs.
Now, masters, draw.

> As they aim their arrows upwards, **MARCUS**, out of earshot of **TITUS**,
> quickly intervenes.

MARCUS
Kinsmen, shoot all your shafts into the court;
We will afflict the Emperor in his pride.

> Instantly the **MEN** form a line aiming their arrows directly over the
> wall into the palace. They shoot.

Marcus, we are but shrubs,
no cedars we, No big-boned men framed
of the Cyclops' size; But metal, Marcus,
steel to the very back, Yet wrung with
wrongs more than our backs can
bear: And, sith there's no justice
in earth nor hell, We will solicit
heaven, and move the gods
To send down Justice for
to wreak our wrongs.

TITUS
Ha! Ha!
Good boy, in Virgo's lap; give it Pallas.

INT. THE PALACE ATRIUM — DAWN

Arrows come whizzing through the open roof. One pierces
DEMETRIUS' raft, which deflates, dumping the sleeping couple into
the water.

Chaos ensues as the rudely awakened guests panic at the attack.
Naked and frightened they crash into one another as they grab their
garments and run for cover.

DEMETRIUS (*reading one of the letters*)
Ha! Ha! It's from Titus! It's from Titus!

DEMETRIUS, dodging the flying arrows, grabs floating arrows from
the pool.

EXT. OUTSIDE THE PALACE — DAWN

The men shoot another round of arrows over a different part of the wall.

INT. PALACE — SATURNINUS' BEDROOM — DAWN

SATURNINUS reads TITUS' letters. Furious, he gets out of bed. While
TAMORA, CHIRON and DEMETRIUS are laughing.

INT. THE PALACE'S HALLWAYS AND COURTYARDS — DAWN

SATURNINUS, in his dressing gown, storms out of his bedroom,
down the hall. He clutches a few of the arrows in one hand, the
opened letters in the other. Chasing after him are an anxious TAMORA
and her two bathrobed sons, still dripping wet from the pool. Servants duck into doorways or flee as he approaches.

The camera also chases after him as he marches furiously through one open courtyard after another, ripping arrows out of paintings, potted plants, wooden statues, out of a dog's behind, etc.

SATURNINUS exits from one courtyard through a pair of double doors.

INT. THE SENATE — MORNING

SATURNINUS, now dressed in a suit, bursts through another set of double doors into the assembly hall, which is filled with the TRIB-UNES. TAMORA and her SONS, also appropriately dressed, follow him into the tense and agitated hall.

SATURNINUS rants and raves as he wildly paces back and forth before his assembly, showing them the arrows and the unrolled petitions.

Concerned that the assembly see her husband so out of control, TAMORA remains stoic as she tries to calm him down.

SATURNINUS
Why, lords, what wrongs are these! Was ever seen
An emperor in Rome thus overborne,
Troubled, confronted thus; and, for the extent
Of equal justice, used in such contempt?
My lords, you know, as do the mightful gods,
However these disturbers of our peace
Buzz in the people's ears, there naught hath pass'd,
But even with law, against the wilful sons
Of old Andronicus. And what an if
His sorrows do overwhelm'd his wits,
Shall we be thus afflicted in his wreaks,
His fits, his frenzy, and his bitterness?

TAMORA
My gracious lord, my lovely Saturnine . . .

SATURNINUS
And now he writes to heaven for his redress:
See, here's "To Jove," this "To Apollo";
This "To Mercury"; this "To the god of war";
Sweet scrolls to fly about the streets of Rome!
   (he tosses the arrows and letters in the air)
What's this but libeling against the senate,
And blazoning our injustice everywhere?
A goodly humour, is it not, my lords?
As who would say, in Rome no justice were.

TAMORA
Lord of my life, commander of my thoughts. . .

SATURNINUS
But if I live, his feigned ecstasies
Shall be no shelter to these outrages:
But he and his shall know that justice lives
In Saturninus' health; whom, if she sleep,
He'll so awake, as she in fury shall
Cut off the proud'st conspirator that lives.

> He violently breaks the arrows over his knee. **TAMORA** puts her arm around him and gently swirls him away from the assembly whose shock at their emperor's behavior is evident.

TAMORA
Calm thee, and bear the faults of Titus' age,
Th'effects of sorrow for his valiant sons,
Whose loss hath pierced him deep and scarr'd his heart;

> Not accepting her excuses, **SATURNINUS** petulantly turns away.

TAMORA (*cont'd*) (*to herself*)
Oh Titus, I have touch'd thee to the quick.

> **AEMILIUS** enters the assembly hall, moving through the throng of **SENATORS** directly to **SATURNINUS**.

AEMILIUS
Take arms, my lords, Rome never had more cause!
The Goths have gather'd head; and with a power
Of high-resolved men, bent to the spoil,
They hither march amain, under conduct
Of Lucius, son to old Andronicus.

> The **TRIBUNES** react noisily to news of the attack, looking to **SATURNINUS** for his response. **TAMORA**, also disturbed by the news, looks to her **SONS**. She then approaches **SATURNINUS**.

SATURNINUS (*to Aemilius*)
Is warlike Lucius leader of the Goths?

> **AEMILIUS** nods gravely. **SATURNINUS** sinks into the throne like a small boy.

> **TAMORA** takes him by the arm and leads him to the antechamber.

SATURNINUS (*cont'd*)
Ay, now begins our sorrows to approach:
'Tis he the common people love so much;
Myself have often heard them say

When I have walked like a private man
That Lucius' banishment was wrongfully,
And they have wished that Lucius were their emperor.

AEMILIUS has followed them but TAMORA signals that he should wait outside the door.

INT. THE ANTECHAMBER — MORNING

TAMORA leads her husband in and then closes the door behind them. They are alone.

TAMORA
Why should you fear? is not your city strong?

SATURNINUS
Ay, but the citizens favour Lucius,
And will revolt from me to succour him.

TAMORA
King, be thy thoughts imperious, like thy name!
Is the sun dimm'd, that gnats do fly in it?
Then cheer thy spirit: for know, thou emperor,
  (*she takes him in her arms*)
I will enchant the old Andronicus
With words more sweet, and yet more dangerous,
Than baits to fish, or honey-stalks to sheep.

SATURNINUS
But he will not entreat his son for us.

TAMORA
If Tamora entreat him, then he will.

She opens the door and speaks to AEMILIUS.

TAMORA (*cont'd*)
Go thou before, be our ambassador:
Say that the emperor requests a parley
Of warlike Lucius, and appoint the meeting
Even at his father's house, the old Andronicus.

SATURNINUS
Aemilius, do this message honourably;
And if he stand on hostage for his safety,
Bid him demand what pledge shall please him best.

AEMILIUS
Your bidding shall I do effectually.

He leaves.

TAMORA
Now will I to that old Andronicus,
And temper him, with all the art I have.

SATURNINUS grabs her hand.

SATURNINUS
Then go successantly, and plead to him.

He pulls her to him and kisses her.
She leaves him alone in the room. He
looks at the letter that AEMILIUS had
handed him bearing news of the
attack and begins nervously pacing
up and down the small room. Sounds
of marching drums and trumpets can
be heard far off.

DISSOLVE TO:
INT. A GOTH TENT — AFTERNOON

LUCIUS paces back and forth in the small tent, reading and rereading
a letter he has just received. Sounds of drums and trumpets still
heard in the distance but a little louder.

EXT. THE PLAINS NEAR ROME — A GOTH CAMP — AFTERNOON

An aerial view of the camp shows a daunting number of tents. An
army of SOLDIERS marches up over the hill, returning to the camp.

INT. THE GOTH TENT — AFTERNOON

LUCIUS hears the loud drums and puts the letter in his breast pocket.
He stares at the Goth overcoat resting on a stool. Abruptly he picks
it up and puts it on as he exits the tent.

EXT. THE GOTH CAMP — AFTERNOON

LUCIUS approaches two of the GOTH LEADERS. They confer. With
their permission he addresses the assembled company.

LUCIUS
Approved warriors, and my faithful friends,
I have received letters from great Rome,
Which signify what hate they bear their emperor,
And how desirous of our sight they are.
Therefore, great lords, be, as your titles witness,
Imperious, and impatient of your wrongs;
And wherein Rome hath done you any scathe,
Let him make treble satisfaction.

GOTH LEADER
Brave slip, sprung from the great Andronicus,
Whose name was once our terror, now our comfort;
Whose high exploits and honourable deeds
Ingrateful Rome requites with foul contempt,
Be bold in us: we'll follow where thou lead'st,
And be avenged on cursed Tamora.

GOTHS
And as he saith, so say we all with him.

INT. LUCIUS' TENT — LATE AFTERNOON

> He and the two GOTH LEADERS are poring over a map of Rome and her environs. A scuffle is heard outside the tent. The LIEUTENANT exits the tent to see what the trouble is.

> The INFANT cries.

> LUCIUS and the GOTH LEADER, curious, also exit the tent.

EXT. THE TENT — LATE AFTERNOON

> LUCIUS is surprised to see AARON brought before him.

> The GOTH SOLDIER who had caught him forces AARON to his knees before LUCIUS.

> AARON looks up at LUCIUS with contempt. He then looks away.

> SOLDIERS have surrounded the kneeling AARON, their rifles aimed directly at him. He keeps his head bowed.

LUCIUS
O worthy Goth, this is the incarnate devil
That robb'd Andronicus of his good hand;
This is the pearl that pleased your empress' eye;
And here's the base fruit of his burning lust.
Say, wall-eyed slave, whither wouldst thou convey
This growing image of thy fiend-like face?
Why dost not speak? what, deaf? not a word?
A halter, soldiers! hang him on this tree,
And by his side his fruit of bastardy.

> LUCIUS snatches the INFANT out of AARON's arms. AARON lunges after him and all the rifles click as the soldiers move in on AARON.

> Meanwhile a noose has been attached to the branch of an army crane.

AARON
Touch not the boy,—he is of royal blood.

Lucius, save the child, If thou do this, I'll show thee wondrous things...

LUCIUS
Too like the sire for ever being good.
First hang the child, that he may see it sprawl,
A sight to vex the father's soul withal.

   He glances at the noose.

LUCIUS (*cont'd*)
Get me a ladder.

AARON
Lucius, save the child,
If thou do this, I'll show thee wondrous things,
That highly may advantage thee to hear:
If thou wilt not, befall what may befall,
I'll speak no more but vengeance rot you all!

LUCIUS
Say on: an if it please me which thou speak'st,
Thy child shall live, and I will see it nourish'd.

AARON
An if it please thee! why, assure thee, Lucius,
'Twill vex thy soul to hear what I shall speak;
For I must talk of murders, rapes, and massacres,
Acts of black night, abominable deeds,
Complots of mischief, treason, villainies
And this shall all be buried in my death,
Unless thou swear to me my child shall live.

LUCIUS
Tell on thy mind; I say thy child shall live.

AARON
Swear that he shall, and then I will begin.

LUCIUS
Who should I swear by? thou believest no god.

AARON
What if I do not? as, indeed, I do not;
Yet, for I know thou art religious,
And hast a thing within thee called conscience,
Therefore thou shalt vow
By that same god, what god soe'er it be,
To save my boy, to nourish and bring him up;
Or else I will discover naught to thee.

LUCIUS
Even by my god I swear to thee I will.

143

He passes the **INFANT** to another **SOLDIER** and returns to hear
AARON's story.

AARON
First know thou, I begot him on the empress.

LUCIUS
O most insatiate and luxurious woman!

AARON
Tut, Lucius, this was but a deed of charity
To that which thou shalt hear of me anon.
'Twas her two sons that murder'd Bassianus;
They cut thy sister's tongue, and ravish'd her,
And cut her hands, and trimm'd her as thou saw'st.

LUCIUS
O detestable villain! call'st thou that trimming?

AARON
Why, she was wash'd, and cut, and trimm'd; and 'twas
Trim sport for them that had the doing of it.

LUCIUS
O barbarous, beastly villains, like thyself!

AARON
Indeed, I was their tutor to instruct them:
That codding spirit had they from their mother,
That bloody mind, I think, they learn'd of me,
Well, let my deeds be witness of my worth.
I train'd thy brethren to that guileful hole,
Where the dead corpse of Bassianus lay:
I wrote the letter that thy father found,
And hid the bag of gold beneath the tree
I play'd the cheater for thy father's hand;
And, when I had it, drew myself apart,
And almost broke my heart with extreme laughter:
And when I told the empress of this sport,
She swounded almost at my pleasing tale,
And for my tidings gave me twenty kisses.

Say, wall-eyed slave, whither
wouldst thou convey
This growing
image of
thy fiend-like
face?

GOTH LEADER
What, canst thou say all this, and never blush?

AARON
Ay, like a black dog, as the saying is.

LUCIUS
Art thou not sorry for these heinous deeds?

> LUCIUS signals for the SOLDIERS to direct AARON to the ladder.

> AARON shrugs them off and makes his own way to the ladder. He climbs to the top.

AARON
Ay, that I had not done a thousand more.
Even now I curse the day—and yet, I think,
Few come within the compass of my curse
Wherein I did not some notorious ill:
As, kill a man, or else devise his death;
Ravish a maid, or plot the way to do it;
Accuse some innocent, and forswear myself;
Make poor men's cattle break their necks;
Set fire on barns and hay-stacks in the night,
And bid the owners quench them with their tears.
Oft have I digg'd up dead men from their graves,
And set them upright at their dear friends' doors,
Even when their sorrows almost was forgot;
And on their skins, as on the bark of trees,
Have with my knife carved in Roman letters,
"Let not thy sorrow die, though I am dead."
Tut, I have done a thousand dreadful things
As willingly as one would kill a fly;
And nothing grieves me heartily indeed,
But that I cannot do ten thousand more.

> AARON takes the noose and places it around his own neck at the top of the ladder. A SOLDIER yanks the rope tight as two others prepare to knock the ladder down.

LUCIUS
Bring down the devil; for he must not die
So sweet a death as hanging presently.

> AARON instantly removes the noose from his own neck, leaps from the top of the ladder and lunges at LUCIUS.

AARON
If there be devils, would I were a devil,

I have
As
And
But

done. a thousand **dreadful things**
willingly as one would kill a fly;
nothing grieves me heartily indeed,
that I cannot do ten thousand
more.

To live and burn in everlasting fire,
So I might have your company in hell,
But to torment you with my bitter tongue!

SOLDIERS restrain him as LUCIUS' foot slams down on top of the handcuff chain, forcing AARON on all fours.

LUCIUS (*overlapping with the end of* AARON's *speech*)
Sirs, stop his mouth, and let him speak no more.

A SOLDIER hits AARON with the butt of his rifle.

FADE TO BLACK.
INT. A GOTH TENT

LUCIUS vigorously washes his face in a small basin. A GOTH SOLDIER enters the tent.

GOTH SOLDIER
My lord, there is a messenger from Rome.

AEMILIUS appears. LUCIUS, totally unnerved by AARON, tries to regain composure.

LUCIUS
Welcome, Aemilius: what's the news from Rome?

AEMILIUS
Lord Lucius, and you princes of the Goths,
The Roman emperor greets you all by me;
And, for he understands you are in arms,
He craves a parley at your father's house,
Willing you to demand your hostages,
And they shall be immediately deliver'd.

GOTH LEADER
What says our general?

LUCIUS
Aemilius, let the emperor give his pledges
Unto my father and my uncle Marcus,
And we will come.

INT. TITUS' HOUSE / BATHROOM — NIGHT

TITUS soaks in a steaming tub in an upstairs room. Ancient leather manuscripts and books litter the floor. A writing board rests on the rim of the tub over his lap. Dabbing a pen into the blood of his amputated wrist, he furiously writes nonsensical words, decrees of vengeance and signs on leaves of paper spread before him.

Who doth
molest my
contemplation?

In front of a red whirling wheel of Boschian demons sits the **GODDESS REVENGE** on the back of a reclining lion-chariot. On her head, like the Statue of Liberty, she wears a crown of daggers. A strip of black gauze hides her eyes, like Blind Justice. Where hands should be she has two coned gauntlets and her huge pendulous breasts form her shield. The voice, though distorted, will reveal that this is **TAMORA**.

From the nipple of the **GODDESS REVENGE** a plastic tube is attached. The end of the long tube feeds smoke into the mouth of **MURDER**, a minister to **REVENGE**, who lounges seductively at her feet. He sports a tiger head as a hat and instead of hands he has two ferocious snapping mouths with immense fangs. This is **DEMETRIUS**.

On the left side of the **GODDESS REVENGE**, perched on the branch of a tree, is **RAPE**, her other minister. His head is enveloped with the outstretched wings of an owl and his naked, muscular body is dressed only in a little girl's training bra and panties. This is **CHIRON**.

INT. TITUS' HOUSE, BATHROOM — NIGHT

NOTE: For a while this "hallucination" will be intercut with TITUS in his bathroom. He will remain in his tub, talking to the window.

TAMORA (*close whispering*)
Titus, I am come to talk with thee.

TITUS (*covering his ears*)
No, not a word.

TAMORA
If thou didst know me, thou wouldst talk with me.

TITUS
I am not mad; I know thee well enough.
For our proud empress, mighty Tamora:
Is not thy coming for my other hand?

TAMORA
Know, thou sad man, I am not Tamora;
She is thy enemy, and I thy friend:
I am Revenge; sent from th'infernal kingdom,
Accompanied by Rape and Murder here
To ease the gnawing vulture of thy mind,
By working wreakful vengeance on thy foes.
Come down, and welcome me to this world's light;
Confer with me of murder and of death.

> TITUS gets out of the tub, dripping wet. He slowly moves to the window and fumbles with his hand and stump to open the window even wider. Perhaps he will jump?

TITUS
Art thou Revenge? and art thou sent to me,
To be a torment to mine enemies?

TAMORA
I am; therefore come down, and welcome me and my ministers.

> TITUS leans out the window.

EXT. BACKYARD OF TITUS' HOUSE — NIGHT

> Looking up we see a long shot of TITUS leaning out the window addressing RAPE, REVENGE and MURDER who appear (to him) to be in the backyard.

TITUS
Good Lord, how like the empress' sons they are!
And you, the empress! but we worldly men
Have miserable, mad, mistaking eyes.
O sweet Revenge, now do I come to thee;
And, if one arm's embracement will content thee,
I will embrace thee in it by and by.

O sweet Revenge

TITUS disappears from the upstairs window.

TAMORA, CHIRON and DEMETRIUS are truly in the backyard wearing outrageous masquerade costumes of RAPE, REVENGE and MURDER. CHIRON leaps down from the branch of a tree to join his mother and brother who are in hysterics over the success of their ruse.

TAMORA
This closing with him fits his lunacy:
Whate'er I forge to feed his brain-sick fits
Do you uphold and maintain in your speeches,
For now he firmly takes me for Revenge;
And, being credulous in this mad thought,
I'll make him send for his son Lucius;
See, here he comes, and I must ply my theme.

The three masqueraders snap into theatrical poses as TITUS emerges from the back door of the house, wearing his bathrobe.

TITUS
Long have I been forlorn, and all for thee:
Welcome, dread Fury, to my woeful house:
Rapine and Murder, you are welcome too:
How like the empress and her sons you are!

Well are you fitted, had you but a Moor:
Could not all hell afford you such a devil?

TAMORA
What wouldst thou have us do, Andronicus?

DEMETRIUS
Show me a murderer, and I'll deal with him.

CHIRON
Show me a villain that hath done a rape,
And I am sent to be revenged on him.

TITUS (*to Demetrius*)
Look round about the wicked streets of Rome;
And when thou find'st a man that's like thyself,
Good Murder, stab him; he's a murderer.
   (*to Chiron*)
Go thou with him; and when it is thy hap
To find another that is like to thee,
Good Rapine, stab him; he's a ravisher.
   (*to Tamora*)
Go thou with them; and in the emperor's court
There is a queen, attended by a Moor;
Well mayst thou know her by thy own proportion,
For up and down she doth resemble thee:
I pray thee, do on them some violent death;
They have been violent to me and mine.

TAMORA
Well hast thou lesson'd us; this shall we do.
But would it please thee, good Andronicus,
To send for Lucius, thy thrice-valiant son,
And bid him come and banquet at thy house;
I will bring in the empress and her sons,
The emperor himself, and all thy foes;
And at thy mercy shall they stoop and kneel,
And on them shalt thou ease thy angry heart.
What says Andronicus to this device?

   TITUS goes to the back door of the house.

TITUS
Marcus, my brother!

INT. LIVING ROOM IN TITUS' HOUSE — NIGHT

   MARCUS, PUBLIUS, CAIUS, SEMPRONIUS and VALENTINE are playing cards when the voice of TITUS interrupts.

TITUS (O.S.)
'Tis sad Titus calls.

> MARCUS lowers his head with a sigh, looks at the others and then rises to go to TITUS.

EXT. BACKYARD OF TITUS' HOUSE — NIGHT

> TAMORA and her SONS, in a panic, lower their heads, trying to hide themselves as MARCUS appears at the back door.

TITUS
Go, gentle Marcus, to thy nephew Lucius;
Thou shalt inquire him out among the Goths:
Bid him repair to me, and bring with him
Some of the chiefest princes of the Goths;
Tell him the emperor and the empress too
Feast at my house, and he shall feast with them.

> MARCUS, recognizing TAMORA and her SONS, is about to protest when TITUS quickly shuts him up with a knowing look.

TITUS (*cont'd*)
This do thou for my love; and so let him,
As he regards his aged father's life.

MARCUS
This will I do, and soon return again.

> He disappears into the house.

> Unnerved at the potential discovery, TAMORA knows it's time to leave.

TAMORA
Now will I hence about thy business,
And take my ministers along with me.

TITUS
Nay, nay, let Rape and Murder stay with me;
  (*starting towards the house*)
Or else I'll call my brother back again.
And cleave to no revenge but Lucius.

TAMORA (*aside to Demetrius and Chiron*)
What say you, boys? will you abide with him,
Whiles I go tell my lord the emperor
How I have govern'd our determined jest?

DEMETRIUS (*aside to Tamora*)
Madam, depart at pleasure; leave us here.

159

Hark, wretches! How I mean to martyr you.

TAMORA
Farewell, Andronicus: Revenge now goes
To lay a complot to betray thy foes.

TITUS
I know thou dost; and, sweet Revenge, farewell.

> He grabs her, pulling her close and kissing her smack on the lips.
> With uncertainty, **TAMORA** leaves.

CHIRON
Tell us, old man, how shall we be employ'd?

TITUS
Tut, I have work well enough for you.

> **TITUS**, again, goes to the back door.

TITUS (*cont'd*)
Come hither, Publius . . .

INT. TITUS' HOUSE — NIGHT

> **MARCUS** is just taking his leave of the men at the front door. He
> halts, as do they all, at the sound of **TITUS'** voice.

TITUS (O.S.)
Caius, Valentine!

> **MARCUS** nods for them to go to **TITUS** as he exits out the front door.

> **VALENTINE** and **SEMPRONIUS** exit the front door after **MARCUS**.

> **PUBLIUS** and **CAIUS** run through the house en route to the back door.

EXT. BACKYARD OF TITUS' HOUSE — NIGHT

> **PUBLIUS** and **CAIUS** exit calmly from the back door.

PUBLIUS
What is your will?

TITUS
Know you these two?

> **PUBLIUS** and **CAIUS** move close to **CHIRON** and **DEMETRIUS**, who are
> very nervous and unaware that **VALENTINE** and **SEMPRONIUS** have
> come around the side of the house and are moving in behind them.

PUBLIUS (*relaxed*)
The empress' sons, I take them: Chiron and Demetrius.

TITUS
Fie, Publius, fie! thou art too much deceived.

The one is Murder, Rape is the other's name;
And therefore bind them, gentle Publius.
Caius and Valentine, lay hands on them.

> Instantly they are surrounded by the four MEN and overpowered after a violent struggle.

> TITUS exits into the house while the BOYS are dragged towards the kitchen.

CHIRON
Villains, forbear, we are the empress' sons.

PUBLIUS
And therefore do we what we are commanded.

> They enter the kitchen.

INT. TITUS' KITCHEN — NIGHT

> TITUS enters and turns back to LAVINIA, who hesitates outside the door.

TITUS
Come, come, Lavinia; look, thy foes are bound.

> A frightened LAVINIA cautiously enters the kitchen. CHIRON and DEMETRIUS, bound and naked, hang upside down suspended from meat hooks. Upon seeing TITUS and LAVINIA, the BOYS whimper through their gagged mouths.

TITUS (*cont'd*)
Now let them hear what fearful words I utter.

> TITUS moves between the two upside-down boys and speaks directly to their heads, which are level with his own.

TITUS (*cont'd*)
O villains, Chiron and Demetrius!
Here stands the spring whom you have stain'd with mud;
This goodly summer with your winter mix'd.
You kill'd her husband; and, for that vile fault,
Two of her brothers were condemn'd to death,
My hand cut off, and made a merry jest;
Both her sweet hands, her tongue, and that more dear
Than hands or tongue, her spotless chastity,
Inhuman traitors, you constrain'd and forced.
What would you say, if I should let you speak?
Villains, for shame you could not beg for grace.
Hark, wretches! how I mean to martyr you.

He reveals a large kitchen knife.

TITUS (*cont'd*)
This one hand yet is left to cut your throats,
Whilst that Lavinia 'tween her stumps doth hold
The basin that receives your guilty blood.
You know your mother means to feast with me,
And calls herself Revenge, and thinks me mad.
Hark, villains! I shall grind your bones to dust,
And with your blood and it I'll make a paste;
And of the paste a coffin I will rear,
And make two pastries of your shameful heads;
And bid that strumpet, your unhallow'd dam,
Like to the earth, swallow her own increase.
This is the feast that I have bid her to,
And this the banquet she shall surfeit on;
And now prepare your throats.—Lavinia, come.

TITUS cuts their throats as LAVINIA moves in to collect the blood in her white basin.

TITUS (*cont'd*)
Receive the blood.
Come, come, be every one officious
To make this banquet; which I wish may prove
More stern and bloody than the Centaurs' feast.

DEMETRIUS and CHIRON have stopped twitching. They are dead.

TITUS (*cont'd*)
So now cut them down, for I'll play the cook,
And see them ready 'gainst their mother comes.

TITUS and LAVINIA exit the kitchen as the KINSMEN go to CHIRON and DEMETRIUS.

INT. TITUS' KITCHEN — BRIGHT SUNNY DAY

Two pies sit cooling on the open windowsill à la "Betty Crocker." A breeze blows the chiffon curtains as birds chirp merrily. The voices of the arriving guests are heard.

INT. THE DINING ROOM — DAY

We follow them into the dining room. The banquet table is laid out. **SERVANTS** stand by to receive the guests.

MARCUS (*continuing*)
The feast is ready, which the careful Titus
Hath ordain'd to an honourable end,
For peace, for love, for league, and good to Rome:
Please you, therefore, draw nigh, and take your places.

SATURNINUS
Marcus, we will.

Everyone sits. **TAMORA** and **SATURNINUS** are seated at each end of the long table.

From behind a red velvet curtain, **TITUS** enters from the kitchen dressed like a cook with a chef's hat. **YOUNG LUCIUS** follows carrying a large pie.

TITUS
Welcome, my gracious lord; welcome, dread queen;
Welcome, ye warlike Goths; welcome, Lucius;
And welcome, all: although the cheer be poor,
'Twill fill your stomachs; please you eat of it.

The pie is placed on the table and TITUS begins to carve it.

SATURNINUS
Why art thou thus attired, Andronicus?

TITUS
Because I would be sure to have all well,
To entertain your highness and your empress.

TAMORA
We are beholding to you, good Andronicus.

TITUS
An if your highness knew my heart, you were.

> TITUS and YOUNG LUCIUS serve TAMORA and SATURNINUS the
> pieces of pie.

TITUS (*cont'd*)
Will't please you eat? will't please your highness feed?

> LAVINIA quietly enters the room, her face veiled. TITUS glances at
> her and then speaks to SATURNINUS.

TITUS (*cont'd*)
My lord the emperor, resolve me this:
Was it well done of rash Virginius
To slay his daughter with his own right hand,
Because she was enforced, stain'd, and deflower'd?

SATURNINUS (*while eating*)
It was, Andronicus.

TITUS (*moving towards Lavinia*)
Your reason, mighty lord?

SATURNINUS
Because the girl should not survive her shame,
And by her presence still renew his sorrows.

> During the following speech **LAVINIA** faces her father, lifts her veil,
> looks into his eyes and revolves her body so that her back leans up
> against his chest. **TITUS** gently places one arm around her upper
> body while stroking her cheek with his one hand.

TITUS
A reason mighty, strong, and effectual;
A pattern, precedent, and lively warrant,
For me, most wretched, to perform the like.
Die, die, Lavinia, and thy shame with thee.

> He quickly breaks her neck. She collapses in his
> arms to the floor.

> Everyone at the table rises, stunned.

SATURNINUS
What hast thou done, unnatural and unkind?

TITUS (*holding Lavinia in his arms*)
Kill'd her, for whom my tears have made me blind.
I am as woeful as Virginius was,
And have a thousand times more cause than he
To do this outrage;—and it now is done.

SATURNINUS
What, was she ravish'd? Tell who did the deed.

TAMORA (*still sitting*)
Why hast thou slain thine only daughter thus?

TITUS
Not I; 'twas Chiron and Demetrius:
They ravish'd her, and cut away her tongue;
And they, 'twas they, that did her all this wrong.

SATURNINUS
Go fetch them hither to us presently.

> **TITUS** reels around the table like a wild lion till he arrives at the pie,
> which he picks up high in the air and then plunks down in front of
> **TAMORA**.

TITUS
Why, there they are both, baked in that pie;
Whereof their mother daintily hath fed,
Eating the flesh that she herself hath bred.
'Tis true, 'tis true; witness my knife's sharp point.

He stabs TAMORA in the neck with the carving knife.

SATURNINUS lunges at TITUS and throws him onto the tabletop.
Plates and glasses fly and crash. Mayhem! SATURNINUS is on top of
the table over TITUS. He grabs the candelabra, bites the burning
candle out of the holder and then plunges the candle spike into
TITUS' stomach. The tablecloth catches on fire.

LUCIUS drags SATURNINUS down the long table.

He then grabs him by the hair and stuffs a large serving spoon down
his throat.

SATURNINUS gags but is not dead. LUCIUS seizes a revolver from the
GOTH PRINCE and, placing the barrel at SATURNINUS' temple, he
pulls the trigger.

The sound of the gunshot reverberates as we pull back to . . .

EXT. INSIDE THE ROMAN COLOSSEUM — NIGHT

. . . reveal the bloody banquet scene, sitting in the center of the colosseum. The bleachers are now packed with SPECTATORS. They are of
many nationalities, races, ages, and they are silent, still.

The GUESTS at the banquet slowly leave the scene of the crime and
move to the front bleachers to sit with the rest of the SPECTATORS.
Only YOUNG LUCIUS is left alone, among the dead.

THE CLOWN appears and, nonchalantly, places clear plastic sheets
over the bodies of TAMORA, LAVINIA, TITUS and SATURNINUS.

In another part of the arena a podium has been erected. MARCUS
stands upon it, addressing the masses over a loudspeaker.

MARCUS
You sad-faced men, people and sons of Rome,
By uproar sever'd, like a flight of fowl
Scatter'd by winds and high tempestuous gusts,
O, let me teach you how to knit again
This scatter'd corn into one mutual sheaf,
These broken limbs again into one body;
Come, come, thou reverend men of Rome,
And take our emperor gently by the hand,
Lucius our emperor; for well I know
The common voice do cry it shall be so.

    LUCIUS mounts the podium.

LUCIUS
Now is my turn to speak.

    He points to **THE CLOWN** who holds **AARON**'s **INFANT** in a small
    cage high in the air (the way he had held **YOUNG LUCIUS** at the
    beginning of the film).

LUCIUS (*cont'd*)
Behold this child,
Of this was Tamora delivered;

If one good deed in all my life I did, I do repent it from my very soul.

The issue of an irreligious Moor,
Chief architect and plotter of our woes.

AEMILIUS
O thou sad Andronici,
Give sentence on this execrable wretch.

> At the far end of the arena **AARON** is being lowered into
> a pit in the ground.

LUCIUS
Set him breast-deep in earth, and famish him;
There let him stand, and rave, and cry for food:
If anyone relieves or pities him,
For the offense he dies. This is our doom.

> **AARON** is now buried up to his neck. Vultures circle around his head.

AARON
O, why should wrath be mute, and fury dumb?
I am no baby, I, that with base prayer
I should repent the evils I have done:
If one good deed in all my life I did,
I do repent it from my very soul.

LUCIUS
Go some of you, bear Saturninus hence,
And give him burial in his father's grave.
My father and Lavinia shall forthwith
Be closed in our household monument.
As for that ravenous tiger, Tamora,
No funeral rite, nor man in mourning weeds,
Nor mournful bell shall ring her burial;
But throw her forth to beasts and birds of prey
Her life was beast-like, and devoid of pity;
And, being dead, let birds on her take pity.

YOUNG LUCIUS stands over the small cage. Slowly he opens it. . . .

The sound of a baby crying transforms into thousands of babies crying, then into squawking birds of prey and then into the tolling of bells.

YOUNG LUCIUS walks away from the crowd, carrying the INFANT in his arms.

As he approaches the archway that leads out of the arena, the night sky slowly gives way to dawn.

THE END

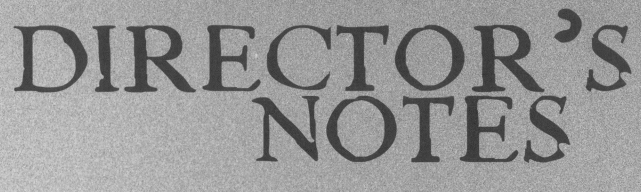

DIRECTOR'S NOTES

"I wanted to blend and collide time, to create a singular period that juxtaposed elements of ancient barbaric ritual with familiar, contemporary attitude and style."

—Julie Taymor

Above: Julie Taymor on the set during filming in Italy. Previous page: Julie Taymor working in the swamps outside of Rome.

For centuries *Titus Andronicus,* Shakespeare's earliest play, has been the subject of hot debate. It was regarded as his most successful potboiler in his own day, and the polite centuries, before our own, were shocked by the juxtaposition of heightened drama, ruthless violence and absurdist black comedy. It is precisely these characteristics that fascinated and convinced me that the play was ripe for adaptation to film, speaking directly to our times, a time whose audience feeds daily on tabloid sex scandals, teenage gang rape, high school gun sprees and the private details of a celebrity murder trial. And equally a time when racism, ethnic cleansing and genocide have almost ceased to shock by being so commonplace and seemingly inevitable. Our entertainment industry thrives on the graphic details of murders, rapes and villainy, yet it is rare to find a film or play that not only reflects the dark events but turns them inside out, probing and challenging our fundamental beliefs on morality and justice.

For *Titus* is not a neat or safe story, where goodness triumphs over evil, but one in which through its relentless horror, the undeniable poetry of human tragedy emerges in full force, demanding we examine the very root of violence and judge its various acts.

War, ritual sacrifice, infanticide, rape, nihilistic torture, honor killing, suicide and vengeance: the ferocious, cynical and wickedly witty voice of the young Shakespeare has created a condemning dissertation on this addiction and basic nature of mankind. The glory and victory of war for one nation is grief and devastation for another. Though at times arguably necessary, once one form of violence is accepted and justified, the floodgates are opened and the reverberations flow into a never-ending vicious cycle.

The Characters: Titus, Tamora and Aaron

The great general Titus Andronicus is a fascinating and unnerving protagonist. At first glance he could be our Colin Powell or General Schwarzkopf. The Roman people, in their love and reverence for their triumphant war hero, beg that he become their emperor in a time of chaos. He is an honourable man, a strict but loving father who respects traditions and the law, but whose fatal flaw is, ironically, this rigidity and inability to adapt to the emotional climate around him. According to religious ritual Titus mercilessly sacrifices the eldest son of the captive Goth queen. This first act is the catalyst for the rest of the events that spiral out of control. From great war hero, Titus descends into a madness that rivals King Lear's. The armour of his worldview shattered, Titus, in his insanity, is finally able to see the world as it truly is. In a bittersweet and wonderfully absurd scene he acknowledges that the Goddess of Justice has fled the earth, so he wraps letters around arrows, shoots them to the heavens, soliciting the gods to right his wrongs. Ultimately Titus weds his sorrow with vengeance, and in a final act of retribution this great general evolves into a mythic pastry chef, serving up his enemies in the form of pies to be devoured by their mother.

Tamora, the Goth queen, could be the precursor for Lady Macbeth. In fact, she is much more dimensional and psychologically comprehensible than Shakespeare's most famous villainess. First seen as captive, she witnesses the brutal sacrifice of her son. After her pleas of mercy fall upon deaf ears, she cries out with searing venom, "O cruel, irreligious piety!" From this moment onwards we understand her motivations and we watch in horror as the lust for vengeance transforms her into the Goddess of Vengeance incarnate. Along the way this extraordinary character moves us as a mother, seduces us as a sexy and sly lover and confounds us with her brilliant and cunning control as the powerful Empress of Rome.

Tamora's slave, lover and cohort in evil is Aaron the Moor. Perhaps the most disturbing and yet contemporary of all the characters,

Julie Taymor directing Anthony Hopkins (Titus) on the set in Rome.

*Original concept drawing from Production Designer
Dante Ferretti of the public steps in front of the Capitol.*

Aaron begins as an enigma. His story unfolds as we watch in shock his master manipulation of the awful events. His nasty sense of humor and his asides to the camera connect the audience to him in the same manner as an Iago or Richard the Third. But what sets him apart from those archvillains is that Aaron is black. Shakespeare has painted a picture of racism that is unparalleled in his other plays. The speeches of Aaron that reflect his fury at the bigoted world surrounding him, and the vile words that spew at him from the rest of the characters, allow us to reflect on how and why he became this godless soul. Nihilistic, atheistic, cold and calculating, this dark figure emerges as the mirror image of Titus. Titus begins as the good man, acting upon honour and a sense of morality. Aaron is the artful and self-aware devil who revels in horrific acts of atrocity without conscience. But by the end, Titus' turn as the cook closely resembles an Aaron act in its cruelty and creativity, while Aaron, the loner, evolves into a loving father, ready to sacrifice himself for the life of his child.

Stylistic Concept

In 1994 I directed an Off Broadway theatrical production of *Titus Andronicus* for Theatre for a New Audience. I became entranced with the play and felt it would lend itself to the medium of film. In adapting *Titus* to a screenplay, the challenge was to maintain the contrasts and scope in Shakespeare's vision: his story and language are at once poetic and very direct, shifting between graphic, base emotions and ephemeral, mythic revelations. Though I was committed to creating a film whose world would be grounded in a sense of possibility and reality, I was also committed to the ideas I had formulated in the theatre that juxtaposed stylized and naturalistic imagery.

Production Design: Location as Metaphor

Modern Rome, built on the ruins of ancient Rome, offered the perfect stratification for the setting of the film. I wanted to blend and collide time, to create a singular period that juxtaposed elements of ancient barbaric ritual with familiar, contemporary attitude and style. Instead of re-creating Rome, 400 A.D., the locations of the film would include the ruins of Hadrian's villa, the baths of Caracalla, the Colosseum, etc., as they are today, with all their corroded beauty, centuries of graffiti and ghastly, ghostly history. As counterpoint to the classical architecture, Dante Ferretti, my production designer, introduced me to E.U.R., Mussolini's government centre, whose principal building is referred to as the "square colosseum" because of its myriad arches. Built by Mussolini to re-create the glory of the ancient Roman Empire, this surreal—almost futuristic—architecture was a setting that perfectly embodied the concept for the film.

To frame the narrative I chose an architectural structure to function in a symbolic manner: the Roman Colosseum; the archetypal theatre of cruelty, where violence as entertainment reached its apex.

The film opens with a prologue that encapsulates the spectrum of "violence" as it transforms, in a matter of seconds, from innocuous entertainment to horrific reality. As a child's innocent play with his toy soldiers escalates into a palpably thunderous explosion of bombs, the boy falls through an "Alice in Wonderland" time warp, right into the Colosseum. Magically his toy Roman soldiers have become armoured flesh and blood, covered in layers of earth—Titus and his armies returning from war with a triumphant march into the arena. The conventions of the film are set in motion: archaic armour and weapons, motorcycles, tractors, tanks and horse-drawn chariots, comfortably jumbled together like the toys on the boy's kitchen table. As to the spectators in the bleachers, there are none. Only the sound of their cheering, as if ghosts of past centuries were being awakened. The boy takes his part as Young Lucius, Titus' grandson, and it is through his eyes that the audience will witness this tale of revenge and compassion.

The scene that follows the opening titles is set in a Roman bath. As the clay streams off the bodies of the soldiers, revealing their skin, the actors transform from mythic sculptures to human beings. In essence, the film moves into a mode of "reality." From here on the film was set in over a hundred locations and only returns to the formality of the Colosseum for the finale.

The Crossroads and the Swamp are two examples of how location functions as ideographs for the thematic essence of a scene.

The Crossroads: At a certain point Titus realizes that his actions have resulted in his responsibility for the potential execution of his own sons. His self-awareness places him at a crossroads in his life, where his worldview begins to unravel. Literally and figuratively, his armour is gone; he is vulnerable. The physical crossroads with its limitless vanishing points underlines his state of mind and his relationship to his family and Rome.

The Swamp: Shakespeare's words suggest it all:

"Here stands the spring whom you have
    stain'd with mud . . ."
"Speak, gentle niece, what stern ungentle
    hands
Have lopp'd and hew'd and made thy
    body bare
Of her two branches . . ."

The swamp is a metaphor for the ravish-

Julie Taymor directing Laura Fraser (Lavinia).

179

ment of Lavinia. She stands deserted, on a charred tree stump, surrounded by muddy waters that gurgle with sulfur springs. Where once were hands are now gnarly twigs. The result is surreal and poetic, thus keeping with my vision of the work and not falling into the trap of utter realism. There is a danger in a literal and graphic portrayal of an image such as Lavinia's dismemberment. It is easily too grotesquely horrific and can upstage the larger picture of the event.

Counterclockwise from above: Line Producer Conchita Airoldi and Production Designer Dante Ferretti; Costume Designer Milena Canonero; Composer Elliot Goldenthal; Film Editor Françoise Bonnot.

Costumes

As in the production design, the blend of styles inspired from three select eras (ancient Rome, the 1930s and the present) was a meticulous procedure on the part of Milena Canonero, the costume designer. The palette of our created world is limited to red, white, blue and black; suggested by the color of veins under pale skin. Metallics, stone and animal furs were also key textures to a design that functions in a metaphoric manner, as with the locations. Costumes were conceived to express the nature of a character, the personality of people and of events rather than to maintain a specific time period.

Titus first appears in blackened, armoured battle dress; a powerful warrior, brutal, invulnerable and rigid in his worldview. As the story progresses and Titus is reduced in pomp and stature to a naked soul, set on the rack of madness, he moves through shades of gray to a final and pristine white. From armour to military uniform to a baggy gray sweater and loose-fitting corduroy pants to a terrycloth robe barely concealing his nudity to his final cook's outfit, we experience through his costumes the journey from great hero to madman to mythic pastry chef. Tamora, like Titus, has a range of costumes that move her from a captive enemy in wet fur and mud to a golden Goth queen in metal and ritualistic tattoos. Her

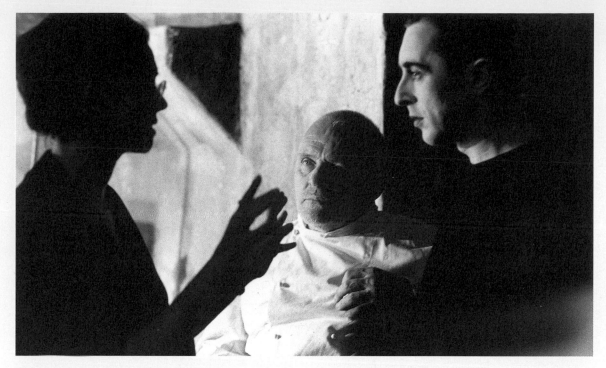

Julie Taymor, Anthony Hopkins and Alan Cumming.

wedding dress plays on her masculine and feminine powers like something out of Visconti's *The Damned* (1930s). Lavinia, on the other end of the scale, is "the jewel of Rome," dressed like a Grace Kelly from the 1950s; little black gloves and a full bell skirt, daddy's little girl all ready for defilement. Even perched on the stump, once ravaged, her bloodied and torn petticoats suggest Degas' ballerina. These references are not literal but suggestive, playing upon archetypes that have become the vocabulary of our times.

The Cast

I was blessed to have a most superb cast for my first feature film. Once Anthony Hopkins agreed to play Titus, the rest of the cast was put into place. Hopkins is well versed in Shakespeare, but he was not particularly interested in doing any more of it. After reading the screen adaptation, he found he was attracted to the darkness of the piece and its grotesque humour. It was a wonderful opportunity for him to place his stamp on the relatively unknown role. Jessica Lange had never done Shakespeare but was drawn to the complex and dimensional role of Tamora, whose entire motivation is set in motion during her first scene. Harry Lennix had played Aaron in the theatrical production I directed Off Broadway. Here was a chance to further explore this compelling character. Alan Cumming, as a neu-

rotic, preening and quixotic despot, seemed a perfect foil for the gravity of Hopkins. Angus Macfadyen, Colm Feore, Laura Fraser, Matthew Rhys, Jonathan Rhys Meyers and the rest of the cast all arrived in Italy with varying degrees of experience in theatre and with Shakespeare in particular. We had a three-week rehearsal period before shooting began, which was instrumental in making the verse natural, comprehensible and poetic on the tongues of the actors. I wanted the language to become second nature. Cicely Berry, a vocal coach from the Royal Shakespeare Company, was invited to work one-on-one with the actors, while I was able to rehearse scenes. This unpressured, intimate time allowed the cast to take tremendous chances, experiment and explore the themes and characters. As we would be shooting out of order, this rehearsal period was also an opportunity to rehearse in order of the script, allowing the actors to discover the through line and arc of their parts.

The Shoot

A good three-quarters of the film was shot on location in and around the city of Rome. The interior sets were shot mostly at the famed Cinecittà studios. Ferretti, with his supervising art director, Pier Luigi Basile, created extraordinary sets for the Senate, the pool

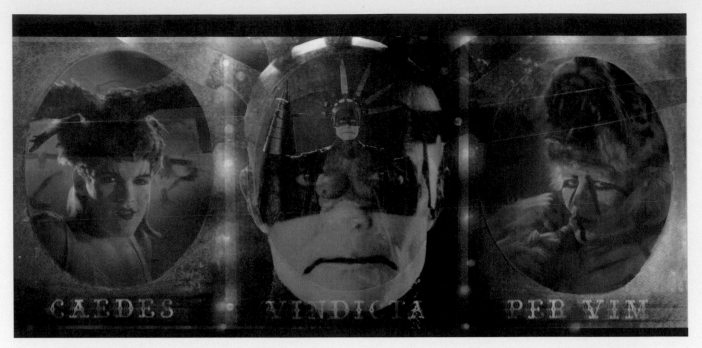

CAEDES · VINDICTA · PER VIM

The Penny Arcade Nightmare of Rape, Revenge and Murder.

atrium, the mausoleum and Titus' house. As the Roman Colosseum does not have a floor and was off-limits for a film shoot, we traveled to Pula, Croatia, where remains a perfectly preserved colosseum from the ancient Roman Empire. We shot the opening and closing scenes for the film in the winter of 1998. Two months later, with the war in Kosovo, this would have been impossible. The irony of shooting these scenes in the Balkans lay heavily on all of us.

Our line producer, Conchita Airoldi, pulled together the terrific (and mostly Italian) crew. The cinematographer, Luciano Tovoli, and I worked together on devising angles and camera movements that would support the rhythm and narrative of a scene. Dramatic, sculptural lighting was important to me, and Luciano was a genius at accomplishing a crystalline, high-contrast style of photography. You can almost see through the eyeballs of Titus in his close-ups.

During the entire shoot Françoise Bonnot, our editor, worked on the film. Her experience ranges from art films to action pictures. I knew she would keep the pacing of the film taut, and yet her understanding of character nuance was impeccable. Once the shooting was finished, it took only about ten weeks to complete the editing. One of the reasons for this was because the shooting style was not to cover every character and scene with the obligatory master shot, medium two shots, singles and reverses. The cutting of many scenes was preconceived with ordered shot lists and storyboards, especially the transitions. And, of course, we did not have the time and money to do extensive coverage on every scene. Sometimes we would suffer from not enough choices, and Françoise would have to work some magic. But basically every scene shot is in the picture due to an extensive amount of discriminating planning and script editing beforehand.

Music

Elliot Goldenthal, in composing his score, followed the same stylistic concepts as the designers. The march into the Colosseum begins with minimalist, primitive percussion, then swells into a full male chorus and sweeping symphonic grandness. The Latin text is a translation from the Shakespeare of the captain's speech announcing the return to Rome of victorious Titus. As we are visually introduced to the Rome of E.U.R., the '30s buildings and the motorcade speeches from the cars of the two princes, his music moves into a boogie-cool jazz amalgam. The muscle of the Senate and the decadence of the wedding party are supported in energy, sexuality and humour with the brass sounds of the big band. For the wild boys, Chiron and Demetrius, and the black humour of Aaron, the music is Goldenthal rock. And the hallucinatory penny arcade nightmares and daydreams move to a carnival madness. Besides the interplay of style, Goldenthal works with the repetition of musical motifs, as in the "pleading theme" that occurs every time a character falls to his or her knees to beg for the life of their child. This helps to underline the larger themes of blood and mercy. As a whole the score is operatic, matching the pitch and fervor of the text.

Envisioning the Violence

My cue came from Shakespeare himself. The genius of his drama is that he juxtaposes very direct, simple and visceral actions with immense poetic verbal imagery, allowing neither direction to overindulge in either gratuitous action or sentimental poeticizing. In contrast to Lavinia's fate, the gruesome action of Titus' hand being lopped off by Aaron with a meat cleaver is in full view: the pain, the scream, the mess of blood, the rags to stop the bleeding—all matter of fact and no fancy. Throughout the film, there is a tension between the real and the surreal, the poetic and the graphic, thus hopefully allowing the adrenaline to rush while the heart and mind are challenged.

Within this very gritty drama there is a constant referencing to Latin and Greek mythology as well as to animal and elemental symbolism. We see the teeth of cruelty and then hear that "Rome is but a wilderness of tigers. . . ." Lavinia, Titus' daughter, is often referred to as a doe, and the rape and mutilation that overcome her are direct parallels to the story of Philomela in Ovid's *Metamorphoses*. These images became quite concrete in my mind and seemed crucial in the physical telling of the tale. Verbal motifs would become visual ones. The image of Lavinia, the doe, being ravished by Chiron and Demetrius, at once both the sons of Tamora and ferocious tigers, had to be realized.

I devised the concept of the "Penny Arcade Nightmares" to portray the inner landscapes of the mind as affected by the external actions. These stylized, haikulike images appear at various points throughout the film counterpointing the realistic events in a dreamlike and mythic manner. They depict, in abstract collages, fragments of memory, the unfathomable layers of a violent event, the metamorphic flux of the human, animal and the divine.

The first P.A.N. is presented through the frozen profiles of Titus and Tamora. In an inferno float the marble body parts representing Alarbus, the son of Tamora who was sacrificed by Titus in a Roman ritual during the first scene of the film. Though the brutal act was never presented on-screen, allowing the audience to imagine the horror, I place my first P.A.N. at a point where seeming tranquillity

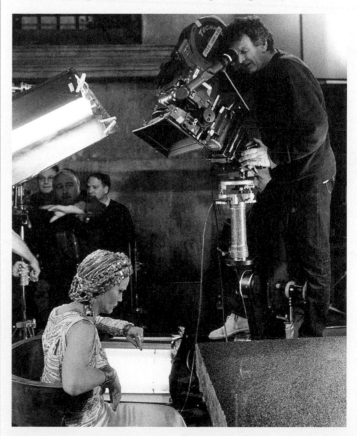

Jessica Lange and Camera Operator Enrico Lucidi.

Julie Taymor directing Anthony Hopkins (Titus) and Jessica Lange (Tamora).

between the enemies, Titus and Tamora, has been established. They are the only persons to "see" the image of the dismembered Alarbus. His sacrifice is the seminal event that propels the train of vengeance throughout the film.

The second P.A.N. occurs when Titus is pleading in the streets for the life of his two innocent but condemned sons. The image of Mutius, Titus' youngest son whom he himself rashly and wrongly murdered in the first act, appears in the form of a sacrificial lamb, evoking the story of Abraham and Isaac. (The head is Mutius and the body is a lamb.) Again, this is to remind us of the inner torment and guilt that has never left Titus. Though the narrative never brings up the event of Mutius' death once it is done, there can be no doubt that it haunts Titus and underlies his pleas for mercy.

The third P.A.N. occurs as Lavinia writes the names of her rapists in the sand. The flashback, depicting the violence by the sons of Tamora, Demetrius and Chiron, is intercut with the furious writing. The approach is not literal. To the onslaught of crazed rock music Lavinia is revealed stripped to her torn petticoats on the top of a truncated column. This ironic image conjures up the reference to a sculptured goddess on a pedestal, as in the

Venus de Milo, soon to be completed with truncated limbs and all. Her head is topped with the head of a doe while her arms are doe's hooves. Demetrius and Chiron—half man, half ferocious tiger—attack and ravish the doe-woman. Leaves fly as wind blows up Lavinia's petticoat, causing her to use her doe arms to keep the skirts down. The famous image of Marilyn Monroe standing over a subway grate and holding her blowing dress down seemed an apt modern iconic parallel adding to this scene of humiliation and rape.

P.A.N. number four comes as stark "reality." A scheme concocted by the crafty and demonic Aaron results in the decapitated heads of Titus' two sons and Titus' own hand being sent back to him in scorn. At this point in the film the violence has escalated to absurd and grotesque proportions. The messenger bearing the "gifts" arrives in a carnival van. Titus, Lucius, Marcus and Lavinia are seated on stools to witness the show. As the metal doors to the van open they are assaulted by the sight of the two heads floating in yellowish liquid in glass specimen jars and the amputated hand draped over a mound of black velvet. Unlike the other P.A.N.s, which were abstract or symbolic representations of an event or psychic state, this P.A.N. is actually happening. This "still life" P.A.N. signals the turn in the play where the nightmares are now reality and madness can be confused with sanity. Order has been replaced with chaos and the road to justice is paved with revenge.

By the fifth P.A.N., Titus has been labeled mad by his enemies and friends alike. In a scene that refers to the classic image of David's painting of Marat, Titus soaks in his bathtub while writing decrees of vengeance with the blood from his amputated arm. A loud knocking disturbs his contemplation, and to the distant strains of carnival music the nightmare of Rape, Revenge and Murder begins. At first the audience should believe that the event is a figment of Titus' tortured mind. Seated on a giant lion is the Goddess Revenge, her crown of daggers reminding us of the Statue of Liberty, while the strip of black gauze that hides her eyes harkens to Blind Justice. Where hands should be she wears two coned gauntlets. Her huge pendulous breasts form her shield, and from the nipple of one of them a plastic tube is attached. This end of the tube feeds smoke into the mouth of Murder, a lounging minister to Revenge who sports a tiger head as a hat. To Revenge's right shoulder perches Rape, her other minister, his head enveloped with the outstretched wings of an owl, his naked body dressed only with a little girl's training bra and panties. Masquerading in these wild and ludicrous costumes are Tamora and her guilty sons Demetrius and Chiron, who have actually dressed up as these mythological characters to torment Titus. Soon it becomes apparent that the masquerade is not a vision but a reality.

By the last of these surreal sequences the line between illusion and substance becomes blurred. The nightmare takes over the plot and madness becomes clarity, preparing us for the worst when the most unimaginable will actually occur.

The finale's banquet slaughter, which mirrors the opening carnage at the boy's kitchen table, ends with Lucius aiming his pistol at the emperor Saturninus. We are in an interior set, Titus' dining room. With the reverberating blast of gunshot, the camera quickly zooms out from the table to reveal the entire scene, minus the walls, now sitting in the center of the Colosseum. This time, the bleachers are filled with spectators. Watching. They are silent. They are we.

As counterpoint to Shakespeare's dark tale of vengeance is the journey of the young boy from childhood innocence to passive witness and finally to knowledge, wisdom, compassion and choice. As the drama comes to its end, Young Lucius, the boy, takes Aaron's baby out of the cage, which sits on the bloodied banquet table. Holding his "enemy" in his arms, Young Lucius begins to move towards the exit arch of the Colosseum. As he walks, the infinite night sky within that single archway slowly gives way to dawn. The boy keeps moving towards the exit, towards the promise of daylight as if redemption were a possibility.

Cinematographer Luciano Tovoli and Julie Taymor.

Acknowledgments

Making films is a collaborative experience, and there are many people who helped me realize my vision for this film. My special gratitude to Jody Patton and Paul Allen for the extraordinary support they gave to a first-time filmmaker, without which I could never have made this movie, and to their helpful staff at Clear Blue Sky Productions, especially Eric Robison, Lee Keller, Jason Hunke, Michael Caldwell, and Co-producer Adam Leipzig; to Anthony Hopkins and Jessica Lange, for their faith in me; to Jeffrey Horowitz, Artistic Director of Theatre for a New Audience, and the superb actors, designers and crew with whom I first mounted the production of *Titus Andronicus* in New York City in 1994; to Ellen and Robbie Little, who were among the first to back my vision for this movie, and whose passion and commitment contributed greatly towards making it a reality, and to their supportive staff at Overseas Filmgroup; to Conchita Airoldi, for her expert handling of all the producing details and demands, day by day; to Bart Walker, my agent, for his steadfast support and guidance, and to his colleagues at ICM; to Karen Thorsen for her thorough expertise and handling of the film in post-production; to Lindsay Law and Fox Searchlight for their important role in launching and distributing the film in North America; to my terrific assistant, Jules Cazedessus, and to these other friends and colleagues who helped to make this film happen: Steven Spielberg, Eileen Gregory, Rick Nicita, Bryan Lourd, Emanuel Nunez, Sandra Marsh, Alessandro Fracassi, Francesca Barra, Peter Frankfurt and Chip Houghton.

Also, my thanks to the many people who assisted us in assembling the materials for this beautiful book, including M. J. Peckos, Karen Lipson, Samantha Crisp, Andrea D'Amico, Doug McClure, Michele Robertson, Nancy Utley, Indika, Leslee Dart, Catherine Olim, Keith Bryant, and Jonathan Bate. Most of all, I am grateful to editors Linda Sunshine and John Jusino, designer Timothy Shaner, the staff of Newmarket Press, and especially to its publisher, Esther Margolis, whose love of the film spurred her to take on this project with much passion and care.

—Julie Taymor, February 2000

Photo credits

Movie photographs by Mario Tursi, Enrico Appetito and Alessia Bulgari unless otherwise noted. The "Penny Arcade Nightmare" sequences were designed and produced by Imaginary Forces/Kyle Cooper. Photos on pages 46-47 and 48-49 by Peter Mountain. Photo on page 171: Deak Ferrand. Drawing on pages 13 and 176-177 by Dante Ferretti. Used with permission. Photos on page 180: Milena Canonero by Brigitte Lacombe; Elliot Goldenthal by Philip V. Caruso; Françoise Bonnot by Patrick Malakian.

Biographies

JULIE TAYMOR's first film, *Fool's Fire*, which she both directed and adapted from a short story by Edgar Allan Poe, aired on *American Playhouse* in 1992. Her first opera direction, Igor Stravinsky's *Oedipus Rex*, which featured Jessye Norman, was also made into a film; it received an Emmy Award and the 1994 International Classical Music Award for best opera production.

She has received numerous awards for *The Lion King*, including two Tony Awards: for best direction of a musical and for original costume designs. She also co-designed the masks and puppets, and wrote additional lyrics for the show, which has productions in New York, Japan, London, and Toronto.

In 1996 Taymor directed *Juan Darién*, which received five Tony nominations. She has also directed *The Flying Dutchman, Salome, The Tempest, The Magic Flute*, and *The Green Bird*.

Taymor has received a MacArthur "Genius" Fellowship, a Guggenheim Fellowship, two OBIE Awards, the first annual Dorothy B. Chandler Award in theatre, and the 1990 Brandeis Creative Arts Award. Other books of her work include *Julie Taymor: Playing with Fire* and *The Lion King: Pride Rock on Broadway*. A major retrospective of Taymor's work opened in the fall of 1999 at the Wexner Center for the Arts in Ohio and is touring the United States.

DANTE FERRETTI, Production Designer, is a five-time Academy Award nominee. His credits include *The Adventures of Baron Munchausen*, Franco Zeffirelli's *Hamlet, The Age of Innocence, Interview with the Vampire*, and *Kundun*.

MILENA CANONERO, Costume Designer, has twice won an Oscar® for her costume designs, for *Chariots of Fire* and *Out of Africa*. Her other films include *Barry Lyndon, A Clockwork Orange*, and *Dick Tracy*.

LUCIANO TOVOLI, Cinematographer, has been the cinematographer for *Desperate Measures, Single White Female*, and *Reversal of Fortune*.

ELLIOT GOLDENTHAL, Composer, a longtime Taymor collaborator, also composed original music for *The Transposed Heads, Juan Darién, The Green Bird*, and *Fool's Fire*. He has received two Academy Award nominations for his film scores, which include *Interview with the Vampire, Michael Collins, Batman Forever, Drugstore Cowboy*, and *The Butcher Boy*. His numerous concert works include an oratorio, *Fire Water Paper*, and a ballet, *Othello*.

FRANÇOISE BONNOT, Editor, won an Oscar® for editing *Z* and is also the editor of such other distinguished films as *Missing, Mad City, A Weekend in the Country, 1492: Conquest of Paradise, Fatman & Little Boy, The Sicilian*, and *The Year of the Dragon*.

CLEAR BLUE SKY PRODUCTIONS' mission is to develop and finance independent film projects that are artistically driven and commercially viable. Their first feature film, *Men with Guns*, was released in 1998. In addition, Clear Blue Sky produced two independent documentary films, *Inspirations* and *Me and Issac Newton*.

OVERSEAS FILMGROUP and its subsidiary, First Look Pictures, specialize in producing quality independent films. Other productions include a preceding Shakespeare film, Ian McKellen's *Richard III*; *A Map of the World*; Virginia Woolf's *Mrs. Dalloway*; Wallace Shawn's *The Designated Mourner*; *The Secret of Roan Inish*; the Oscar®-winning *Antonia's Line*; and *Waking Ned Devine*.

CAST
(in order of appearance)

Young Lucius ....OSHEEN JONES
Clown ....DARIO D'AMBROSI
Titus ....ANTHONY HOPKINS
Tamora ....JESSICA LANGE
Alarbus................................RAZ DEGAN
Chiron ....JONATHAN RHYS MEYERS
Demetrius ....MATTHEW RHYS
Aaron ....HARRY LENNIX
Lucius ....ANGUS MACFADYEN
Quintus ....KENNY DOUGHTY
Mutius ....BLAKE RITSON
Martius ....COLIN WELLS
Priest ....ETTORE GERI
Saturninus ....ALAN CUMMING
Bassianus ....JAMES FRAIN
Marcus ....COLM FEORE
Aemilius ....CONSTANTINE GREGORY
Lavinia ....LAURA FRASER
Little Girl ....TRESY TADDEI
Nurse......................GERALDINE McEWAN
Infant ....BAH SOULEYMANE
Publius ....ANTONIO MANZINI
Caius ....LEONARDO TREVIGLIO
Sempronius ....GIACOMO GONNELLA
Valentine ....CARLO MEDICI
Goth Leader ....EMANUELE VEZZOLI
Goth Soldiers ....HERMAN WEISKOPF
CRISTOPHER AHRENS
Goth General ....VITO FASANO
Goth Lieutenant ....MAURIZIO RAPOTEC
Roman Captain ....BRUNO BILOTTA

FILMMAKERS

Directed by ....JULIE TAYMOR
Screenplay by ....JULIE TAYMOR
Adapted from *Titus Andronicus* by WILLIAM SHAKESPEARE

Produced by ....JODY PATTON
CONCHITA AIROLDI
JULIE TAYMOR
Executive Producer ....PAUL G. ALLEN
Co-Executive Producers ....ELLEN LITTLE
ROBERT LITTLE
STEPHEN K. BANNON
Co-Producers ....ADAM LEIPZIG
MICHIYO YOSHIZAKI

Music Composed by ....ELLIOT GOLDENTHAL

Cinematography ....LUCIANO TOVOLI AIC ASC

Production Designer ....DANTE FERRETTI

Costume Designer ....MILENA CANONERO

Editor................FRANÇOISE BONNOT A.C.E.

Casting ....IRENE LAMB
ELLEN LEWIS

Associate Producer ....KAREN L. THORSON
Co-Associate Producers ....MARK D. BISGEIER and
BRAD MOSELEY

Production Supervisors ....PINO BUTTI and
DINO DI DIONISIO

Supervising Art Director ....PIER LUIGI BASILE
Associate Costume Designer ......NICOLETTA ERCOLE
Set Decorator ....CARLO GERVASI

Production Manager/
Associate Producer ....ROBERT BERNACCHI

Consulting U.S. Producer ....LINDA REISMAN

Unit Production Manager ....GIAN PAOLO VARANI
Unit Managers ....MARCO GRECO
MARCO OLIVIERI
Location Manager ....BARBARA PETRELLI
Camera Operator ....ENRICO LUCIDI
Focus Puller ....LORENZO TOVOLI
Clapper/Loader ....DANIELA CHIOFFI
Trainee..........................SAMBA KOSCHAK
Video Assist ....GIORGIO TOSO

B Camera/Steadicam Operator ..MASSIMILIANO TREVIS
Focus Pullers ....RAFFAELE CHIANESE
ERIC BIGLIETTO
Clapper/Loader ....ANDREA QUAGLIO

Choreographer ....GIUSEPPE PENNESE
Additional Fight Choreography ....DAVID S. LEONG

Voice Specialist ....CICELY BERRY

Dialogue Coach ....CONSTANTINE GREGORY

Dramaturgical Research ....KATHERINE PROFETA

Casting Associate ....MARCIA DeBONIS
Casting (Rome) ....SHAILA RUBIN

Art Directors ....MASSIMO RAZZI
DOMENICO SICA
Assistant Art Directors ....DIMITRI CAPUANI
ROBERTA CASALE
Draftsman ....LUCA TRANCHINO

Assistant Set Decorators ....ALESSIA ANFUSO
BARBEL ELISABET KREISL
MARIA RITA CASSARINO
Draperies ....ROBERTO CINGOLANI
BARNABA PAGLIARINI
Set Dressing Props ....CARLO AVVISATO
CLAUDIO VILLA

Wardrobe Master ....MARCO SCOTTI
Workshop Supervisor ....EMANUELE ZITO
Wardrobe Assistant ....MARIELLA DIRINDELLI
Mr. Hopkins's Dresser ....ARTHUR ROWSELL
Illustrator ....MAX ROTUNDO

Workshop Master	SALVATORE SALZANO
Lead Cutters	ANNIE HADLEY
	ALMA BARBIERI
Cutter	ALBERTO EUSEBI
Shoemaker	AMERICO DE ANGELIS
Seamstresses	ANGELA ANZIMANI
	ANNA ORAZI
	ANNA MARIA LIBERATI
	LUCILLA SIMBARI
	MARIA CARMELA MENGHI
	PIERA CIMINO
	FRANCESCA DI DOMENICO
Armorer	GIUSEPPE CANCELLARA
Assistant Armorers	SALVATORE MANCA
	ATTILIO RUFFINI
	MAURO MOSCATELLI
Sound Mixer	DAVID STEPHENSON
Sound Maintenance	COLIN WOOD
Cable Operators	YISHAI CASTEL
	ALESSANDRO ROLLA
Propmaster	ETTORE GUERRIERI
Propman	GIOVANNI FIUMI
Prop Assistants	LUCIANO AURILIA
	MARIA LAURA ARTINI
Arms/Weapons	FEDERICO ANGELI
	NICOLA CABIATI
Prosthetic Devices	SERGIO STIVALETTI
	LUIGI ROCCHETTI
	GINO TAMAGNINI
Mechanical Devices	GERMANO NATALI
Sfx Supervisor	RENATO AGOSTINI
Sfx Technician	CLAUDIO QUAGLIETTI
Animal Wranglers	LE CARROZZE D'EPOCA SRL.
	ZOO GRUNWALD DI P. MARTINO
	LEIBOVICI DI DANIEL BERQUINY
Key Grip	ROBERTO EMIDI
Best Boy Grip	ROBERTO BAGALÀ
Grips	VALTER PAVIA
	PAOLO FRASSON
	LUCIANO MICHELI
	MARCO SANTARELLI
Gaffer	CARLO VINCIGUERRA
Best Boy	MARCO CONTALDO
Electricians	CLAUDIO FROLLANO
	SPARTACO SARDINI
	GIOVANNI TANCREDI
	SIMONE LUCCHETTI
	IGNAZIO MACCARONE
1st Assistant Directors	ANTONIO BRANDT
	GUY TRAVERS
Co-1st Assistant Director	VANJA ALJINOVIC
2nd Assistant Director	BOJANA SUTIC
3rd Assistant Directors	HENRIQUE DE ARAUJO LAPLAINE
	GILLES CANNATELLA
	LUIGI SPOLETINI
Crowd Marshall	SILVANO SPOLETINI
Stunt Coordinator	STEFANO MIONI
Transport Captain	ROBERTO LEONE
Script Supervisors	RACHEL GRIFFITH
	MARTA GATTI
	DANUTA SKARSWESKA
Key Make-Up Artists	LUIGI ROCCHETTI
	GINO TAMAGNINI
Make-Up Artist	ENZO MASTRANTONIO
Assistant Make-Up Artist	JANA CARBONI
Ms. Lange's Make-Up Artist	DOROTHY PEARL
Key Hair Stylists	MAURO TAMAGNINI
	GIUSI BOVINO
Hair Stylist	MARIA PIA CRAPANZANO
Assistant Hair Stylist	PAOLA GENOVESE
Production Coordinator	NORMA MARIE MASCIA
Assistant To Ms. Airoldi	LETIZIA BALLARINI
Assistant To Mr. Hopkins	TERRY ROWLEY
Assistant To Ms. Taymor	ELEONORA WALSH BALDWIN
Production Secretary	CLAUDIA MOSCATELLO
Urania Pictures Secretaries	SABRINA ANGELUCCI
	MARIA ADELAIDE RICCIONI
Production Assistants	EMILIO ZACCARIA
	FABIO DI DIONISIO
	FRANCESCA CUALBU
	FRANCESCO ZANGARA
Wardrobe P.A.	ROSSELLA PALMA
Wardrobe Assistants	COSTANZA BASTANTI
	GABRIELLA LOUISE LORIA
	MICAELA TENTARELLI
Production Controller	SANDRA NIXON
Production Accountants	SERGIO BOLOGNA
	GIORGIO TREGNAGHI
	ANNA ORIETI
Assistant Accountant	CARLO CAPUTO
Payroll Accountant	CARMELA COMPAGNONE
Location Accountant	MARINA GRAPPELLI
Accounting Assistants	PATRIZIA PIERUCCI
	STEFANO SPARTI
Union Liaison	PAOLO CARTA
Unit Publicist	LINDA GAMBLE, McDONALD & RUTTER
International Publicity	McDONALD & RUTTER
U.S. Publicity	MPRM PUBLIC RELATIONS
Still Photographers	MARIO TURSI
	ENRICO APPETITO
	ALESSIA BULGARI
Construction Manager	LUIGI SERGIANNI
Chief Plasterer	GIUSEPPE LA ROCCA

Head Painter .... BRUNO RANIERI

1st Assistant Editor .... BILL HENRY
2nd Assistant Editor .... SARA THORSON
Apprentice Editor .... IAN HOCHBERG
Assistant Editors .... EDWARD NADALIN
BOB ALLEN
ARMANDO FENTE
ANTONELLA LOMBARDI
DANIELE SORDONI

Music Produced By .... TEESE GOHL
FOR GOHL/McLAUGHLIN
WITH ELLIOT GOLDENTHAL

Conductors .... STEVEN MERCURIO
JONATHAN SHEFFER

Orchestrators .... ROBERT ELHAI
ELLIOT GOLDENTHAL

Electronic Music Producer .... RICHARD MARTINEZ

Recorded & Mixed By .... JOEL IWATAKI

Recording Studios .... ABBEY ROAD, LONDON
MANHATTAN CENTER, NEW YORK

Orchestra Contractor .... ANDY BROWN

Featuring ... LONDON METROPOLITAN ORCHESTRA
THE MASK ORCHESTRA
THE PICKLED HEADS BAND

Saxophone .... BRUCE WILLIAMSON

Guitar .... PAGE HAMILTON
MARK STEWART

Additional Engineering ..... LAWRENCE MANCHESTER
STEPHEN McLAUGHLIN

Music Preparation .... VIC FRASER
Music Editors .... MICHAEL CONNELL
TODD KASOW
DARYL KELL
CURTIS ROUSH
Supervising Sound Editor/Sound Design .... BLAKE LEYH
ADR Supervisor .... DEBORAH WALLACH
Dialogue Editors .... KIMBERLY McCORD
Sound Effects Editor .... GLENFIELD PAYNE

Supervising Foley Editor .... BENJAMIN CHEAH
Foley Editors .... TIM O'SHEA
JENNIFER RALSTON
Foley Artists .... MARKO COSTANZO
JAY PECK
Foley Mixer .... SKIP LIEVSAY
Assistant Sound Editors .... ALEX SOTO
CHRIS FIELDER
DEBORA LILAVOIS
IGOR NIKOLIC
Apprentice Sound Editor .... MATT TAYLOR

Foley Engineer .... GEORGE LARA

Post Production Coordinator .... PETER PHILLIPS
Post Production Accounting .... TREVANNA POST
Taymor/Goldenthal Coordinator .... JULES CAZEDESSUS
Editing Room Assistant .... ANNA DI NUOVO

Visual Effects .....PEERLESS CAMERA COMPANY LTD,
LONDON
Visual Effects Supervisor .... KENT HOUSTON
Visual Effects Producer .... SUSI ROPER
Computer Graphics Animation .... DITCH DOY
TIMOTHY OLLIVE
MARK TWINAM-CAUCHI
PAUL DOCHERTY
ANDREA ADAMS
ARNON MANOR
Digital Compositing .... STEPHEN CUTMORE
PATRICK WONG
JOHN SWINNERTON
Digital Matte Painting .... ERIC CHAUVIN
Additional Digital Compositing .... DIGISCOPE

Penny Arcade Nightmare Sequences Designed And Produced
By IMAGINARY FORCES/KYLE COOPER

Imaginary Forces .... MICHELLE DOUGHERTY
SARA MIRANDI
MICHAEL JAKAB
LORI FREITAG-HILD
CLYDE BEAMER
ROB TRENT
LAUREN GIORDANO
JASON WEBB
MARCUS HUTCHINSON
ROD BASHAM
HOLLY KEMPNER
KEITH BRYANT

Pop Film & Animation .... DEAK FERRAND
BOB WIATR

Main Title Sequence Designed And Produced By
BIPACK, INC./ALEX G. ORTOLL

Sound Editing By C5, INC.

Re-Recording Sound Services Provided By
Skywalker Sound, A Division Of Lucas Digital LTD.,
Marin County, California

Re-Recording Mixers .... GARY SUMMERS
LORA HIRSCHBERG
Re-Recordist .... JENNIFER BARIN
Mix Technician .... JUAN PERALTA
Machine Room Operator .... GABRIEL GUY
Audio Digital Transfer .... JONATHAN GREBER
CHRISTOPHER BARRON
JOAN MALLOCH
Video Services .... CHRISTIAN VON BURKLEO
JOHN TORRIJOS
Negative Cutter .... MO HENRY
Dolby Sound Consultant .... DAN SPERRY

Dailies Timer .... STEFANO GIOVANNINI
Color Timer .... DALE GRAHN

Shooting Services In Croatia .. JADRAN FILM D.D. ZAGREB
Production Manager .... BORIS DMITROVIC
Assistant Production
   Manager .... PREDRAG VOJNOVIC PAJO
Unit Manager .... RANKO GANIC
Production Secretaries .... KLARA DOKMANOVIC
                     VAJNA SIKIRICA
Accountant .... JOSIP BOLJKOVAC
Assistant Director .... ZDRAVKO MADZAREVIC
Crowd Marshall .... ANTUN CACKOVIC
Art Director .... IVO HUSNJAK
Wardrobe Assistants .... DRAGO HABAZIN
                    ANICA SVILAR
Make-Up Artists .... HALID REDZEBASIC
                   ANA BULA
                   JIC
Hair Stylists .... JOLANDA BUHIN
               STEFANIJA ROSSO
Grips .... ANTUN GORISEK
              BRANKO CAVRIC
Electricians .... JOSIP MARSIC
            SIME KNEZEVIC
            SAMIR KADRIC
            JURE KOSTIC

Fiscal Consultant .... STUDIO ROSSETTI
Legal Services .... STUDIO CAU MORANDI
             MINUTILLO TURTUR
             SLOSS LAW OFFICE
Safety Consultant .... NICOLA NICOLETTI
Insurance .... CINESICURTÀ – ROMA

Still Lab .... FAST PHOTO SERVICE SNC
Costumes .... GP 11
             ANNAMODE
             TIRELLI
             NORI
Shoes .... POMPEI
Arms .... RANCATI
Jewelry .... LABA
Wigs .... ROCCHETTI

Set Dressing .... I.C.A.
             M.R.B.
             V.A.E.
            SECURITY CIEMME
            F.B. ARREDAMENTI
            UGO FLAVONI,
            E. RANCATI
            MINCIOTTI & FIGLI
            SANCHINI
            DITTA NUNZI AUGUST
            S.A.P.A.L. SPORT BILIARDI
            CINEARS
            DITTA LATOUR & FIGLI
    ARTIGIANA TAPPEZZIERI E ARREDATORI
            DI BRUNO SCHIAVI
            CREATIVA
            LEO PARETTI
Transportation .... CINETECNICA

Cameras .... CINECAMERAS
Greenery .... NUOVA ROSSIELLO
Lamps & Gels .... REC
Shipping .... INTERNATIONAL MOVIE SERVICE
Negative .... EASTMAN KODAK

This motion picture was filmed in Rome, Italy,
and on location in Pula, Croatia.

With special thanks to:

Theatre for a New Audience:
Jeffrey Horowitz, Artistic Director;
and the original Designers, Cast, and Crew
of the theatrical production of
Titus Andronicus, 1994.

Bart Walker, Steven Spielberg, Eileen Gregory,
Rosalie Swedlin, Rick Nicita, Bryan Lourd,
Emanuel Nunez, Sandra Marsh, Alessandro Fracassi,
Francesca Barra, Peter Frankfurt, and Chip Houghton,
Roger Arar/Loeb & Loeb LLP,
Giovanna Trischitta, Tino's International Travel Service, Inc.

Eric Robison, Lee Keller, Zoe Melendez,
Jason Hunke, and Michael Caldwell.

The Mayor of Rome
Comune Di Roma–
Dipartimento Politiche Culturali–Ufficio Cinema,
Soprintendenza Archeologica per il Lazio per Villa Adriana,
Sovraintendenza ai Beni Culturali –Museo della Civiltá Romana,
Soprintendenza Archelogica di Roma per Villa Dei Quintili,
Museo Nazionale delle Arti e Tradizioni Popolari di Roma,
Soprintendenza per I Beni Ambientali e Architettonici di Roma,
Ente Regionale Parco dell'Appia Antica,
Ente Autonomo Esposizione Universale di Roma,
Università Agraria di Manziana

Archeological Museum of Istria, Pula
Motocycle Club "Twin Horn," Pula
Police Academy, Zagreb

Fendi, American Italian Lloyd, Pignatelli, R. Salato,
Xacus, Walford, MTS, Tabru, Crespi, Ratti

Soundtrack available on Sony Classical

The Producers declare that no animals
were injured during filming.

A Titus Productions Ltd. and
Urania Pictures Co-Production
Copyright © 1999 Clear Blue Sky Productions
All Rights Reserved.

Released in North America by Fox Searchlight.